Dec 21
July 22
Feb 23

Minna's Patchwork Coat

Written and illustrated by

LAUREN A. MILLS

LITTLE, BROWN AND COMPANY
NEW YORK   BOSTON

Copyright © 2015 by Lauren A. Mills

Lyrics from "Great Big House" used with permission from World Around Songs

Little, Brown and Company

Hachette Book Group
1290 Avenue of the Americas, New York, NY 10104
Visit us at lb-kids.com

Little, Brown and Company is a division of Hachette Book Group, Inc.
The Little, Brown name and logo are trademarks of Hachette Book Group, Inc.

The publisher is not responsible for websites (or their content)
that are not owned by the publisher.

First Edition: November 2015

Library of Congress Cataloging-in-Publication Data

Mills, Lauren A., author, illustrator.
    Minna's patchwork coat / written and illustrated by Lauren A. Mills. — First edition.
        pages cm
    Summary: In the poverty of the Appalachian coal country in 1908, eight-year-old Minna's life gets even more difficult after her father dies of black lung, and that winter she cannot go to school because she does not have a coat—until the quilting mothers make her a coat using pieces of cloth from their own lives, each with a special story behind it.
    ISBN 978-0-316-40621-5 (hardcover) — ISBN 978-0-316-40622-2 (ebook) — ISBN 978-0-316-40618-5 (library edition ebook) 1. Children of coal miners—West Virginia—Juvenile fiction. 2. Coats—Juvenile fiction. 3. Quilting—Juvenile fiction. 4. Poor families—West Virginia—History—Juvenile fiction. 5. Community life—West Virginia—History—Juvenile fiction. 6. Elementary schools—West Virginia—Juvenile fiction. 7. West Virginia—History—Juvenile fiction. 8. Appalachian Region—History—Juvenile fiction. [1. Coats—Fiction. 2. Quilting—Fiction. 3. Family life—West Virginia—Fiction. 4. Community life—West Virginia—Fiction. 5. Schools—Fiction. 6. West Virginia—History—To 1950—Fiction. 7. Appalachian Region—History—20th century—Fiction.] I. Title.
    PZ7.M63979Mi 2015
    813.54—dc23
    [Fic]

                                                                        2014040298

10 9 8 7 6 5 4 3 2 1

RRD-C

Printed in the United States of America

For my daughter,
Evie May,
who has the
spirit of Minna

Contents

Chapter 1

The Right Way of Thinking

You never really know what cabin fever is until you have lived in a one-room cabin during a long winter spell. My favorite cure for the cabin fever was riding in the back of the Millers' hay wagon to church, but I remember one bitter wintry morning when I knew Mama was of the mind to say we weren't going.

"Just too darn cold on Rabbit Ridge. God will understand. There's been enough sickness in this house," she was saying to Papa on her way out to the chicken coop.

I was tapping my foot and thinking hard about a way I could shift the winds a little bit to make sure we got out in that hay wagon. An idea came. I lifted Clemmie up onto my hip to do the wiggle dance with me. He was not even three, but he took my directions all right, especially if it meant something fun.

"Minna, what the devil has gotten into you? You're jumpin' and hoppin' around like Lucifer has got a hot poker at your heels!" said Papa, looking up from stoking the woodstove.

"We are the HOPkins family, Papa, and we got the fever," I said, pinching Clemmie's little sausage toes to make him giggle and wiggle some more.

"Is that right? What kind of fever?" Papa was smiling now, and I loved it when he smiled.

"Cabin fever," I said, and started wiggling like a worm. I put Clemmie on the floor so I could start the scratching. "We got the itch, the stitch, the palsy, and the gout, and we are itchin' all over to just git out!"

Mama had just come in the door, a basket of eggs and the cold air with her. "Itchin' or no, we can't go. It's just too darn cold outside for the

Hopkins family today, and Minna's got no coat." There. She had said it.

"Now, Marcy Hopkins, that ain't the right way of thinkin'," said Papa, coughing a little and trying real hard not to. "Nothin' is too much for the Hopkins family. Look here, Jeremy Miller will be drivin' his hay wagon right up to our door, and we ain't going back on my word. We're gonna be in that wagon like I told him, whether the weather be cold or whether the weather be hot!"

"We'll weather the weather whatever the weather, whether we like it or not!" I chimed in, finishing the rhyme for Papa because he was starting to cough again. He had the miner's cough from working too much in the coal mines, and it had nothing to do with the weather.

Papa had a sparkle in his eye. "Minna, fetch me that empty feed sack."

I ran to the pantry, quick as a bunny, and brought the burlap feed sack to Papa.

He scooped up Clemmie from the floor with one big hand and gave him to Mama. "Now, Mama, git your cape and wrap it around you and Clemmie. And I'll just grab your Pinwheel quilt, the one with all the nice bright colors in it," he said, swinging it over his shoulder.

I knew just why Papa loved that quilt best. Working down in the black coal mines all the time meant he hardly ever saw the day or any color but black, and Papa loved bright colors. Now, with the world just white with snow, Mama's colorful quilt was even more of a happy sight to him.

Papa knelt on the wooden floor with the feed sack at his boots and said, "And now, Minna, I want you to hop into this sack. I know it's no coat, but it'll do until I get you the finest coat anyone on Rabbit Ridge ever saw."

I did just as Papa said and hopped into the sack, and he scooped me right up. I was more like a happy, squealing piglet than a bunny. Even

Mama laughed. Right then we heard the Millers' horses neighing as they were coming up the hill, and I knew we were going to ride in that wagon.

Mr. and Mrs. Miller were sitting up front with their daughter, Souci, who was seven like I was, but she went to school and I didn't, and that's why she put on airs. She looked at the feed sack I was in and rolled her eyes. My not having a coat was what kept me from being able to go to school, but I was expecting Souci to be happy that I was going to church, feed sack or not.

"Why doesn't Souci like me, Papa?" I whispered in his ear.

He whispered back. "It's because she doesn't really know you, that's all. When you get a coat, you'll go to school and have lots of friends. You'll see."

Mr. Miller jumped out to give us a hand. "Good to see you can finally make it to church, Jack," he said, slapping Papa on the back, making him cough again. Mr. Miller helped Mama settle onto the hay with Clemmie, and then held me in the feed sack so Papa could get in.

"Minna, I better not let you get too close to our horses, or they might think that orange braid you're nibbling on is a carrot, and they'll want to do the same!" Mr. Miller said, laughing.

I spit my braid out of my mouth and held it tight, but then I saw Papa laughing, so I smiled. I didn't like being teased about my hair, but at least Mr. Miller hadn't called it "red, like the devil," the way some of the boys had. I reckoned that if Papa first noticed Mama on account of her red hair, someday somebody as great as my papa would notice me.

Mama, Clemmie, Papa, and I all huddled under Mama's Pinwheel quilt. We were nice and comfy in the hay of the open wagon, with the cold wind nipping just my nose. I looked up at my papa, feeling warm and happy. "I think I'm warmer than if I *had* a coat, Papa," I told him with all honesty.

Papa looked down and squeezed me. "Minna, you got the right way of thinkin'. People only need people, and nothin' else. Don't you forget that."

Whenever Papa said not to forget something, he really meant it, so I made sure to store what he told me like I would if I had found a silver dollar or an arrowhead or something real special I would want to keep in my box of treasures.

"People only need people," I repeated, and I saw Papa wink at Mama.

Chapter 2

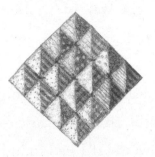

Pay Them No Mind

While Mr. Miller was hitching up his horses in the churchyard, Souci jumped out and didn't even look back. She ran up to Lottie Smith, who was wearing the prettiest coat with an even prettier fur collar. The two of them went into the church together, hand in hand. I saw Clyde Bradshaw and Kevin Baker throwing snowballs at each other behind their parents' backs. Kevin pointed at me in the feed sack, probably thinking I looked like a baby in my papa's arms. He started snickering, which made Clyde laugh, too.

I was giving them my snake eyes and would have stuck my tongue out if Mama hadn't said sharply, "Minna, pay them no mind. The worst punishment you can give is to pretend they aren't there, like they don't matter. You don't want their bad behavior to rub off on yours."

"Mama's right, Minna," said Papa, squeezing me tighter. "They want you to get mad, so don't give them what they want. The more you ignore them, the more they'll make fools of themselves and get into worse trouble."

I didn't want to ignore them. I wanted them to get to know me and like me. But I did my best to pretend they weren't there, and sure enough, it happened just as Papa said it would. Inside church we were all singing "Amazing Grace," one

of Papa's and my favorites, and I could hear the boys behind me snorting and kicking my bench. I just sang louder. Then I heard Kevin Baker say, "Redheaded witch!"

Ooh, was I boiling, and I so wanted to turn around, but I held on to my hymnal like it was a fish trying to squirm away. The next thing I knew, Kevin Baker's father was grabbing him by the collar and Clyde Bradshaw's mama grabbed him, and those boys were marched right out of church, as red as beets. I turned just enough to see the goings-on from the corner of my eye.

I was so glad I had not made a fuss, because then I might have gotten into trouble, too, and it would have spoiled our whole trip. Nope, this was one day that went right with the Hopkins family.

Chapter 3

Little Bear, Little Bear

That winter I remember waking up to the wrenching sound of Papa coughing. I confess that sometimes I liked the sound, because it meant Papa had to be home with us and not down under the earth in the coal mines that might eat him up like they did other papas. His cough meant that he was up closer to the sun and was clean and not covered in black soot all over except for two white circles around his eyes. And being with us meant that no more of the black coal dust was getting into his lungs. Maybe then he'd have a chance to just cough it all out and be well again.

One morning when the snow had melted, Mama put the kettle on and was frying eggs and leftover corn bread, and Papa was sitting in his rocking chair by the window enjoying the sunlight streaming in.

"Mornin', Sunshine," he said, smiling.

I gave him a big hug and buried my face in his chest. I whispered to those black lungs inside of him, "Please get all clear and well."

Clemmie came running over and wanted to be part of the hug. "Come on, Clem," I said. "We got work to do."

"No, I want to play!" He stomped his little bare foot, though it hardly made a sound.

"Well, we have to make you a toy first, and you are going to help me make it."

"Oh, Minna, I really need you to finish carding that pile of cotton," said Mama, desperation creeping into her voice. "I have to get that order done."

Since Papa had been sick with the miner's cough, Mama had worked day and night making quilts to pay for our food. My job was to comb out the weeds in the cotton stuffing that went inside the quilts.

"You two are keepin' lots of folks warm, even if I can't give 'em coal to heat their homes," Papa would say, but he wasn't happy about it. If he wasn't playing his banjo, he just stared out the window from his rocking chair. I think he was trying to catch up on all the sunlight he had missed.

"I can card the cotton today," Papa said. "Let Minna play with Clemmie."

Mama looked doubtfully at Papa. I was the expert carder in the house.

"It won't take Clemmie and me long, Mama. I need to find him something to do so he doesn't get his sticky hands in all that cotton. He makes my job harder."

I had made a doll for myself from Mama's scraps and stuffed it with fluffs of cotton. I called her Fifi and talked to her like she was my

friend, since I didn't have any others. Clemmie didn't count, being my little brother and most times a pest. The last toy Mama made for him had fallen apart, so I was thinking maybe I would make him a new friend to play with.

"How about if I make you a little bear to play with, Clemmie?"

"Will it bite me?"

"Nah, only if you want it to."

So a bear it was. Papa helped me draw it, and Mama fixed it into a pattern that I could pin to the cloth and cut out. She showed me just how I should stitch it.

Clemmie was twirling in circles, he was so happy. When I finished sewing most of the bear, I left an opening for Clemmie to stuff the cotton inside.

Then Papa played his banjo for us. He didn't sing much because it made him cough, so we just sang louder as Clemmie stuffed his bear.

"Little bird, little bird, fly through the window,
Little bird, little bird, fly through the door,
Little bird, little bird, fly through the window,
Hey diddle, hi dum, day.

"Take a little dance and a hop in the corner,
Take a little dance and a hop on the floor,
Take a little dance and a hop in the corner,
Hey diddle, hi dum, day."

But then Papa had us change it to "Little bear, little bear, hop through the window." And we also changed "Mary wore a red dress" to "Minna wore a green dress."

And "Poor old crow sittin' on a tree" to "Poor li'l bear, skinny as can be."

Papa said, "Clemmie, as you're stuffing the insides of that bear, you tell it all the things you hope it might be."

Clemmie's chubby little fingers poked the

19

cotton into the head, and he whispered to the bear, "You be nice and not bite, but if you see a bad bear coming for me, then you bite him."

"How about Li'l Bear just telling Big Bear to go away?" I asked Clemmie.

Clemmie shook his head no.

Then Li'l Bear was finished, and we all took turns kissing it to make it "come alive." I looked from Mama's face to Papa's face to Clemmie's, feeling so happy, like all was right in the world. It was another special thing I would have put in my treasure box for safekeeping, if I could have.

Chapter 4

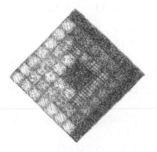

If That Mockingbird Don't Sing

The spring air seemed to make Papa feel better. He was awfully busy around the house, mending old boards that had come loose, gathering firewood, and making plans to build a bigger garden and barn. Mama just shook her head, but she was smiling to see Papa so full of life.

One morning Papa grabbed the Log Cabin

quilt Mama had made and told me to put on my boots. "Minna, you're coming with me. We've got business with Aunt Nora."

Aunt Nora wasn't really an aunt, but everyone called her that. I guess because she was like everybody's aunt. She was the healer and midwife on the mountain and had delivered a lot of us on Rabbit Ridge. Most folks called on her if they were sick or hurt instead of going down into town to see the doctor. But some folks were afraid of Aunt Nora, saying she was a Cherokee witch with powers she shouldn't be using.

"How come Aunt Nora's so smart about the plants, Papa? Is it because she's old?"

"She's not that old," said Papa. "Her face has just seen a lot of sun."

Mama looked curiously at Papa and said, "That's gonna be a steep walk back for you. Why don't you let me go get what you need, so you don't have a coughing fit?"

"I'll manage. I have Minna with me," Papa said, and I felt so proud. Poor Clemmie was crying in Mama's arms because he couldn't come with us.

I called back to him, "Clemmie, watch over Fifi for me, and I'll find a present for Li'l Bear!" He smiled and nodded through his tears.

Walking down the mountain through the woods, we could hear Mama's pretty voice fading. She was singing,

"Hush, little Clemmie, don't say a word,
Minna's going to buy you a mockingbird.
If it can't whistle and it can't sing,
Minna's going to buy you a diamond ring."

"Minna, you know what's worth more than a diamond ring?" Papa asked me, adjusting the quilt under his arm so he could hold my hand.

"Yep. Mama's singin'," I said, because that's what he always told me.

"Yep, and your voice, too. No diamond ring can do what a pretty song can. You keep singin' and don't ever stop, okay?"

"Okay, Papa," I said, squeezing his hand.

When we reached Aunt Nora's cabin, we saw her grandson, Lester, in the yard, pulling clay pots out of a shallow pit dug in the ground. His skin was even darker than Aunt Nora's, and he seemed big for being just nine years old. Papa explained that Lester and Aunt Nora had made the pots from the clay they dug up from the riverbank. The pots had been hardening in the fire pit and were now cool enough for Lester to lift them out and hard enough to be usable. Lester nodded a hello to us and pointed to the house. I hadn't heard him speak a single word since he had come to live at his grandma's.

Aunt Nora opened the door before we could knock. Maybe that's the kind of thing that made some people call her a witch. She didn't seem like the ones I had heard about, though. She was short

with a face that was brown like old leather. Her eyes were as black and shiny as marbles, and I liked looking at them. But I was a little nervous, too. I started sucking on the end of my braid, until Papa pulled it out. He and Mama were always trying to break me of that habit, but my mouth and braid had minds of their own.

"Whatcha have there, Jack?" Aunt Nora asked, first staring at my face, then eyeing the quilt I was now holding, as if she had just laid eyes on something that sparkled. It seemed she could hardly keep from touching it. "A Log Cabin quilt? Is this one of Marcy's?"

Papa nodded and I handed it to her. We went inside, and she looked it over real careful, studying all the tiny stitches, and I knew she liked it. "You must want something pretty big for this," she said. "I've already given you my best medicine, and I'm not sure my ginseng tincture is gonna fight black lung. It will take a lot more."

"I'm not asking for more medicine. I've come to ask help from your boy," said Papa, surprising both Aunt Nora and me.

"What do you want with him?" she asked, quickly putting the quilt down, as if it were full of poison.

I looked around the cabin at all the herbs and baskets hanging from the beams and at the clay pots on the shelves. I knew Lester could help Aunt Nora with her medicines and beehives, and he could make and sell pots, and garden, and milk goats, and shear sheep, but what was it Papa wanted?

"I want to grow more plants, especially squash, beans, and pumpkins. And I'll need your boy's help adding on to our chicken barn and putting up a fence." Papa wiped his forehead and coughed.

"I suppose you'll be asking for a couple of milking goats next, won't ya?" asked Aunt Nora with one eye squinting. She didn't seem to feel sorry for Papa, and mostly she didn't seem to trust him. Everybody trusted Papa.

"Well, that, too," said Papa, scratching his head. "And I have another bargain to offer you." Papa started coughing again and looked around the room for a chair.

Aunt Nora pulled up a stool for him and ordered, "Give it a rest while I brew up some tea. Minna, grab me a twig of those herbs hanging there."

"The peppermint?" I asked. She nodded but seemed surprised that I knew the plant. Peppermint was one of my favorite herbs that Mama grew in our garden. I saw a mama rabbit and her babies cuddled under it because the strong smell hid the rabbits' smell from other animals. I kept their secret from Mama as long as I could and always told her I would collect the peppermint.

Aunt Nora's tea was a mix of ginger, sassafras, slippery elm bark, peppermint, and honey to soothe Papa's throat. I think she slipped some ginseng root in there, too. Her concoctions always worked like magic, and I watched Papa, waiting to hear him sigh.

Papa sipped the tea and sighed with satisfaction. I smiled.

"So, what's this other bargain you've got?" asked Aunt Nora.

"Well, Minna can come down here and help you garden and wild craft and such," said Papa. He saw the frown on Aunt Nora's face and quickly added, "She could teach you and Lester how to read, too. In return for the reading lessons and the quilt and Minna helping with your plants, you would give me a couple of milking goats, let me borrow Lester for some farm help, and then you'd teach Minna about your herbal medicines."

"Humph," said Aunt Nora. "My people have their own alphabet, and that's what I use. And

29

besides, I've never taught any white folk before. It might weaken me to give away what I know."

I must have raised my eyebrows, because Aunt Nora patted my knee and said, "But I think of you, Minna, more like one of the little folk of the forest than one of the white folk. It's just that it's somethin' I got to think about. I was passing what I know on to Lester, though he doesn't seem as interested in it as I had hoped. He sure would like to know how to read—more of your language, that is." She looked at Papa and said, "But Minna doesn't go to school. How does she know how to read?"

I sat up tall. "Mama taught me, and her mama taught her! My grammy is a smart schoolteacher in Asheville! We have three books at home: the Bible, a book of poetry, and a book of fairy tales," I said proudly.

"Well, now, that seems like almost all a body would need," said Aunt Nora. "Can you write, too?"

"I sure can! And Papa is going to get me a

fine coat so I can go to school this fall. I'll come down here after school and tell Lester the lessons I learn."

"Is that so? You would do that?" Aunt Nora studied me for a while, then said, "Lessons like that may come in handy. There's not a school for coloreds or Indians for miles, and I wouldn't dare even try to send him to the Rabbit Ridge school-house. He would get beat up, and someone might set our cabin on fire."

Papa rubbed his chest and said, "Now, I don't think the folks on Rabbit Ridge would do such terrible things."

"Even so, we'd have to keep the reading lessons a secret," said Aunt Nora, looking at me sternly, and I nodded vigorously. "I just might try this out for Les's sake, but mind you, Jack, the minute this little white girl puts on airs around Lester, the bargain is over, you hear? He's been through enough. He's a smart boy, as smart as any white boy. So we'll just see, you understand? We'll just see."

Papa looked at me and said, "Teaching a colored boy might even be a risk for you and our family, Minna. Are you willing to take that risk, and can you keep it a secret if need be?"

"Cross my heart and hope to die," I said, crossing my heart with my finger. "I can keep a secret, and I'm not afraid of *anyone*."

"People you thought were your friends might call you bad names," added Aunt Nora.

"Only sticks and stones can break my bones. Names can never hurt me." Grammy had just sent me such poems in the mail, and I was happy to have a chance to share them.

Aunt Nora chuckled and said, "I like your spirit, little one, but you'll learn someday how names *can* hurt, sometimes just as much as sticks and stones."

Chapter 5

Asking and Thanking

Aunt Nora called out the door, "Les! Jack Hopkins has something he wants to ask you!" Then she took my hand and we went outside. "I'm going to teach you your first lesson, Minna." She led me to some very pregnant sheep and said, "Do you see what they're munching on?"

Along the fence was a raspberry patch. The

goats and sheep were carefully picking off the leaves and chewing them. "Those leaves will help strengthen them when it comes time to deliver their babies. They'll help with the nursing, too," said Aunt Nora. "The sheep know it without any medicine woman like me telling them. We were once like that, too. Now only some of us know the secrets of the plants. Most everything I know, I learned from my *elisi*. That's the Cherokee word for grandma on the mother's side, and what Lester calls me. Anyway, my *elisi* learned what she knew from her father, my great-grandfather, who was the shaman for his people."

I didn't know what a shaman was, but I was afraid Aunt Nora might think I was stupid if I asked.

"My *elisi* was his only child, and she had the *gift*. So he taught her what he knew, and then she, too, had the power to understand the messages of the plant spirits."

My eyes grew big. I wanted that gift so badly.

"Elisi was pregnant with my mother when our people were marched off our land by the government. So many thousands of Indians died on that long march, they called it the Trail of Tears. I bet you know nothing about it."

I shook my head no.

She took a deep breath. "Well, Elisi didn't

want to lose that baby inside of her, so she and my grandpa hid up in these mountains and raised their daughter and then me besides." Aunt Nora looked up at the trees. "Elisi was very wise. She taught me to sit and listen to each plant's spirit tell its story. Sometimes the story doesn't seem to make sense at first," she said, laughing. "But if you listen hard and are patient, soon you know what that plant can do. It's more like remembering than learning." She looked very stern and pointed her wrinkled finger at me and said, "I always ask permission before I pick it; and I always thank it. Otherwise, it's not a gift and won't work. That's how it is in plant spirit medicine."

She stopped, so I nodded to show her I understood. Then she continued.

"The Cherokees say that long ago, when the world first began, all of creation spoke the same language. The plants spoke with the finned fish, the four-legged creatures spoke with the

36

stones and wind, and the most helpless, poorest creatures—the two-legged humans—also spoke with the plants, stones, and other animals. All the rest knew that if the pitiful two-legged ones were to survive, they would need help. So the plants and animals that knew they were better suited to survive than the humans gave of themselves as willing sacrifices. All that the two-leggeds had to do was ask permission."

Aunt Nora pointed her finger at me again and said, "But the two-leggeds grew to feel more important than the others. They acted as if all of life circled around *them*. They forgot to ask permission." Aunt Nora's gaze went out to the valley and beyond, where the mountains met the sky.

"What happened?" I asked.

"The animals grew angry because the two-leggeds took more than they needed, never asking. The plants grew angry, too, for all the trampling, digging, cutting, and burning, and all the while the two-leggeds never asked or cared how much they disturbed the harmony of the land. As a punishment the animals sent the humans diseases. But the plants felt sorry for the humans and said, 'For every sickness, we will grow the cure. All the humans have to do is listen when we talk to them.'"

She mumbled something to the raspberry bush that sounded like a thank-you, and picked off a leaf and gave me some to taste. "Asking and thanking, that's how it works, and how it works for everything. If everyone knew that, we'd be a happier nation."

I nodded. The raspberry leaf didn't taste very good, but I tried not to make a face.

"I want to listen," I said. "Can you teach me? What plants help my papa the most?" I asked.

"Oh, lots of them, and sometimes it's the bunch of them working together. I've given him wild cherry bark and ginger for the coughing, and ginseng and goldenseal root and the five-finger plant for his disease. But you know, the plant spirits aren't happy with man digging down inside Mother Earth and burning her bones," Aunt Nora grumbled, but then saw my worried face.

"Don't mind my talk, Minna. Your papa is a good man doing what he can for his family. But if the Great Spirit needs him, the Great Spirit will take him. You must remember that nothing ever really dies, and nothing lasts forever, either. Everything always changes, and knowing that helps us be brave. We just go on our journeys and do the best we can wherever we are." She patted my head and said, "You're a good listener, little one, but that's enough lessons for today."

Chapter 6

Soft Stuffing

As Aunt Nora and I headed back to the house, I picked off a little sheep's wool from the fence.

"Aunt Nora, would it be all right if I took a bit of fleece home for my little brother?" I was remembering my promise to Clemmie and thinking he could scrunch the wool into a little ball and pretend it was a lamb.

Aunt Nora smiled, showing all her beautiful white teeth. Her eyes disappeared into half-moon slits. "Sure you can take it," she said, "and I have something special to go with it." When we walked up the porch steps, we heard Lester playing the banjo for Papa, but he stopped as soon as we came in.

"That's all he wants to do, is play music," said Aunt Nora. "His grandpa taught him."

Lester nodded and smiled at the mention of his grandpa.

"Simon taught me, too. You don't get a finer teacher than that," said Papa.

Aunt Nora pulled a little wooden lamb and kid goat down from the shelf and placed them in my two palms.

"Oh, these are beautiful," I said, and they were. I loved them at once. "Did *you* make these, Aunt Nora?"

"Yes, I did," she stated proudly, "and now they'll have a new home. One for you and one for your brother. You choose."

"I can't take anything so fine...and something you made yourself," I said, even though I really wanted that little goat, and I knew my doll, Fifi, would want it, too.

"Friends share," said Aunt Nora, "and we are friends, don't you think?"

"Oh, yes, but...I don't have anything like this that I can give *you*," I said, all worried.

"Your gift of friendship is more than enough," said Aunt Nora, patting my shoulder and nodding at Papa. Papa nodded back, and his eyes twinkled.

I gave Aunt Nora a big bear hug, which seemed to surprise her at first, but then she hugged me back. I looked over at Lester, and he got all embarrassed and looked down at his banjo, pretending to tune it. Maybe he was worried I was going to hug him, too. He had nothing to fret about. I would *never* hug a boy, except for Clemmie.

As we were heading out the door, Papa said to Lester, "And don't forget to bring the banjo up, Les." Then he turned to Aunt Nora and explained, "A little playing during the breaks makes the work go easier."

Aunt Nora shook her head with a smile and lightly swatted Papa's back as we stepped off the porch.

When we were walking up the path homeward, Papa said, "Aunt Nora can be a snapping turtle at first, but like a turtle, she has a hard shell on the outside only to protect how soft she is on the inside."

"Mm-hmm," I agreed.

"So, what did Aunt Nora teach you?"

"Askin' and thankin' is how everything works,"

I told him, "and raspberry leaf is good for nursing and delivering. Aunt Nora said her great-grandpa was the shaman for her people and taught what he knew to her grandma 'cause she had the *gift*. Papa, I was too embarrassed to ask Aunt Nora what a shaman is."

Papa said, "Minna, never be embarrassed to ask about something you don't know. How else will you learn? A shaman is like a minister and a doctor in one. He figures out how to heal people and tells them whatever it is they need to know."

"I thought so. Papa, did you know about the Trail of Tears?" I asked, holding tight to his hand. He walked a whole lot slower up the path than he had going down.

We stopped and Papa rested against a birch. "Yes, I've heard of it. The government kicked the Indians off their land and marched them a long, long way out west."

"And lots of people died on the way," I added.

"Papa, I remember Aunt Nora's husband. He was white, but I don't remember what happened to him."

Papa sighed. "That's one question you were right not to ask Aunt Nora. You must have been about four, almost five, when he died, so we didn't want to tell you. Simon Jenkins was a great man and banjo player, the best I've ever heard. Yes, he was white and farmed with Aunt Nora, but when their grandson, Lester, lost his parents and came to live with them, it was a hard time to get by. So Simon started working in the coal mine to bring in more money. Aunt Nora didn't want him to, but he did it anyway 'cause we'd had such a bad year of weather for the crops. Simon was killed in the same mining accident that killed Clyde Bradshaw's pa almost three years ago. It was hard on Aunt Nora, and more so on Lester, since he had lost his ma and pa in that same year."

"Lester is all Aunt Nora's got left of her family," I said sadly. It didn't seem fair for that to happen to someone who was always asking and thanking. "Papa, how did Lester's parents die?"

"Ya know," said Papa, taking out a handkerchief from his overalls pocket, "no one ever really heard that story. I'm not so sure Aunt Nora even knows or wants to know. Her daughter married a Negro man, and they lived close to the city. I don't think things went easy for them, since her daughter looked more white, like her pa. Negroes have it hard enough, but for one of them to marry someone who is white or looks white can be pretty hard for people to accept." Papa looked out across the hills. "Sometimes it's worse to be half of one thing and half of another. To each side you're the other color, so in the end you belong nowhere. People just can't see past the different-colored shells we wear on the outside. If they could, they'd know that we're all made up of the same stuff on the inside."

"Soft stuffing," I added.

Papa chuckled and cleared his throat. "Soft

stuffing," he repeated. "Minna, I'm going to find you a coat with soft stuffing on the inside."

"I hope it's a coat with lots of colors on the outside," I said. "Then *everybody* would have something to like!"

"You got the right way of thinking, Minna Hopkins." Papa took my hand and said, "Shall we?"

We went on up the mountain. I went first, sometimes pulling Papa.

Chapter 7

Rabbit's Invitation

The next day Aunt Nora and Lester came up to our cabin. Lester started to work with Papa right away, and Aunt Nora took me back down to her place. She had me picking the sheep's wool from the briars and picking other leaves as she pointed out the medicine plants and told me their stories of healing, or stories like how the strawberries came to be. She told me how the mockingbird remembers and mimics all the sounds he hears and then sings them to his girlfriend to impress her with how much he knows of the world.

"He's hoping that she'll choose him for her mate," Aunt Nora said. "Sometimes he'll sing to her way into the fall just so she'll remember him in the spring. Some say," said Aunt Nora in her quiet, mysterious voice, "that the mockingbird only mocks, but the truth is that when the forest is quiet, he mixes the melodies of all he knows and comes up with his own beautiful song. And if by chance you hear that song, then you are *blessed.*"

"Is that what you learned from your *elisi*?" I asked.

"Nah, I learned that one myself," Aunt Nora said proudly.

I filled one whole feed sack with bits of wool. Aunt Nora caught me putting a mockingbird feather into the sack once, but she didn't scold me for it—only nodded.

"You like pretty things?" she asked.

I nodded. "Doesn't everybody?"

"Some more than others, I suppose," she said.

"I can't wait for Papa to get me a pretty coat to wear to school this fall."

"So how come you don't go to school with the others now?"

I shrugged.

"Your ma and pa need your help at home?" She was looking at me square in the face with her dark, midnight eyes. Her brown, wrinkled hands never stopped moving, as if her fingers had eyes of their own.

"I'll be going to school as soon as I get my new coat. Papa's gonna make sure it's a beautiful one with lots of colors and soft stuffing inside. I hope it has a fur collar, too, like Lottie's. Hers is mink, but I wouldn't mind possum."

"Humph," Aunt Nora scoffed. "I bet the possum wouldn't mind Minna's red braid for its tail."

I felt my face grow hot, and I held tight to my braids.

"Do you know the story of why Possum's tail is bare?" Aunt Nora asked.

I shook my head no.

"Well, a long time ago Possum had a long, beautiful, bushy tail instead of that ugly, bare, ratlike tail. He was so proud of it that he would brush it all day long and sing about it all night. Rabbit was getting tired of hearing Possum's bragging and decided to play a trick on Possum. Rabbit was a little jealous of Possum's tail because Rabbit's tail had been pulled off by Bear."

"Ouch," I said, trying to imagine a rabbit with a long tail.

"Well, there was going to be a big celebration for all the animals. Rabbit told Possum he would send Cricket down to comb his tail before the party.

"So Cricket hopped on down to Possum's. 'Just stretch out and shut your little eyes, and I will make your tail shine bright,' Cricket told Possum. Cricket combed the tail and wrapped a string around it to make it smooth," Aunt Nora said, pointing her finger at me, "but all the while he was clipping off the hair, right to the roots!"

I gasped, "Oh, no!" I put my braid in my mouth and began sucking.

"Yes, he did," said Aunt Nora, "and you better take your braid out of your mouth, or you'll munch all your hair away and have a ratty-looking tail, too." I dropped my braid fast, and right then I was forever cured of sucking on it.

"So what happened next?" I asked.

"That night, when Possum went to the party, he loosened the string on his tail and began his bragging: 'Oh, look at my beautiful tail.'" Aunt

Nora did a little twirl. "'See its beautiful color! Look how it sweeps the ground,' he sang, but then he noticed that all the animals were laughing at him! He swung his head round and saw that his tail was now as ugly and as bare as Rat's. He was so shocked he rolled over on the ground and stuck his feet in the air, helpless. And that is what Possum does to this day when he is taken by surprise."

"Huh. I thought he was just playing dead so no one would bother him," I said.

"That's the Cherokees' tale," stated Aunt Nora.

"Not the Possum's tail?" I asked with a little smile, hoping Aunt Nora would know I was making a joke.

She laughed and said, "It's a tale of a tail."

"I do like the tale," I started to say, "but it was mean of Rabbit and Cricket to do that to Possum. Rabbit should have known how awful it is to lose a tail. Besides, I don't like to think of rabbits as being mean."

Aunt Nora led me to another patch of briars, and the sheep and goats followed us. "Minna, there *is* meanness in the world, and not everyone acts fairly or as we would like," she said. "Sometimes it's better to go about quietly and unnoticed so you don't attract enemies."

I thought about this. "Well, maybe that's why rabbits have brown fur, so that they can hide better by blending in with the brown leaves. If I had a coat of rabbit fur, I could hide from my enemies, but I wouldn't want anyone to kill that many rabbits just for my coat. I like rabbits."

"Maybe Rabbit is your totem," Aunt Nora said.

"What's a totem?" I asked.

"It's a friend and helper…a spirit guide. It's usually an animal that you share things in common with. Sometimes the totem gives you messages. Do you ever dream about rabbits?"

"I think I have," I said. "Sometimes I like to hop like a rabbit." I showed Aunt Nora my hopping skills, and she laughed as she untangled the brambles that had caught on my dress. They made another rip that Mama would make me mend. My dress was getting full of patches.

"A rabbit totem is good for a medicine girl like you, Minna. It can show you cures and also teach you how to face your fears. Sometimes people invite Rabbit to make the things they are most afraid of come true so they will grow and become stronger."

I stopped picking the wool and looked at Aunt Nora, worried. She stared back into my eyes and must have seen my worst fears dancing in them. I looked away. "I don't want Rabbit as my totem."

Aunt Nora gave my shoulder a pat. "Rabbit doesn't make hardships happen, but when they do come, she is there to show you how to face them."

I looked up again. Aunt Nora's eyes were soft. All I could think that Rabbit might show me was hopping away or hiding in a hole in the ground. Neither one sounded very brave.

As if she could read my mind, Aunt Nora said, "Rabbit may be small and not as strong as Panther or Bear, but that is why Rabbit is even braver, for she faces danger every day." Aunt Nora peered up at the clouds.

"But Rabbit gets caught and eaten up all the time," I said.

"Do you see rabbits everywhere?" she asked.

"I do."

"Rabbits do well, and they give us a great gift of their life when we are hungry. Rabbit will be your friend, and she will be there when you need her. Now, should we go up to see how Lester and your pa are doing?"

Chapter 8

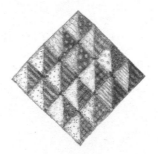

When Twilight Is Fading

Lester was a big help to Papa, and Papa was so grateful to him that at the end of each day he would say, "Don't know what I'd do without you, Les."

Lester would just shrug and say, "It was nothin'."

And Papa would always say, "Lester, you are

somethin'. And don't you forget that!" They would take a lot of breaks and play their banjos. Papa was teaching him "Turkey in the Straw," which he had learned from Lester's grandpa Simon, but I think Lester had already learned it from his grandpa, too, and was just being polite. He sure could play well, just as good as Papa. Aunt Nora and Mama liked to sing along and sometimes play the dulcimer and tambourine, but they also liked just to laugh at Clemmie and me dancing to the tunes.

Lester was still too shy to talk to me. Aunt Nora told me not to mind and that it was just because of all he had gone through. She also said that Lester didn't trust white children, especially girls, ever since some girls in town had been rude to him. I would smile at Lester when I could and tried to be extra funny when I danced to their tunes so that he would laugh. And when he did, Aunt Nora would wink at me. She said he hadn't laughed in a long time.

Somehow Mr. Miller and Mr. Hunter heard about Papa and Lester building the fence and barn and making the garden bigger, and so they came down to help, too. They knew Papa was too weak to do much work. Mr. Miller brought his horses, and they turned the soil over. They helped us add to our few apple trees, and they gave us seeds to plant a garden of corn, potatoes, squash, peas, beans, tomatoes, lettuce, herbs, okra, pumpkins, broccoli, and zucchini. Then all the men and Lester—and sometimes even Shane, Mr. Hunter's ten-year-old boy—would play music at the end of the day. We couldn't wait until music time. I never saw Mama smile so much.

Sometimes Papa would turn to Mama and me and have us sing Grammy's song that she had brought over from Wales called "Dacw nghariad," a sad sweetheart song. I liked singing the Welsh words because they sounded like magic spells. And if Aunt Nora wasn't feeling shy, she would

sing us a Cherokee song. "The Corn Dance Song" was one of my favorites.

But Papa always wanted to end the day singing a favorite of his called "The Ash Grove," even though Mama moaned that it was too sad. We all gathered round and sang it in harmony.

"The ash grove, how graceful, how plainly 'tis speaking,
The harp through it playing has language for me.
Whenever the light through its branches is breaking,
A host of kind faces is gazing on me.
The friends from my childhood again are before me,
Each step wakes a mem'ry as freely I roam.
With soft whispers laden the leaves rustle o'er me,
The ash grove, the ash grove alone is my home.

"Down yonder green valley where streamlets meander,
When twilight is fading, I pensively rove,
Or at the bright noontide in solitude wander,

Amid the dark shades of the lonely ash grove.
'Twas there while the blackbird was cheerfully singing,
I first met that dear one, the joy of my heart;
Around us for gladness the bluebells were ringing,
But then little thought I how soon we should part."

Everyone would stay until the sky turned pink and purple and the trees were black against it, and then they'd pile into Mr. Miller's hay wagon to go home. I'd stay on the porch with Papa, rocking in his chair and listening to all of them singing "Amazing Grace" through the woods until their voices faded.

On one spring night Papa said, "As long as we can still hear the song, echoing through the gloom, we can stay right here, rocking on the porch."

"I can still hear it, Papa," I kept saying. I don't know if I heard it in my mind or if I really heard it, but I do know I liked cuddling with Papa. I told my ears to hear what they could because I didn't want any of it to end.

Papa laughed and said, "Now, Minna, you couldn't possibly be hearin' them singin'. They're all long gone and in bed snorin', and we should be, too."

Chapter 9

A True Midwife

On the days when it was just Lester working with Papa, Mama would sometimes make them stop early when she heard Papa coughing. She would say, "Time for Lester's reading lessons." We'd take out the books and the slate Mama used for teaching me. She would guide me on how to teach Lester to read and write, but in truth I think she was doing most of the teaching. Lester liked Mama and wasn't shy talking to her.

We were both surprised that Lester already knew quite a bit. He knew his numbers better than I did, anyway. And it wasn't long before he was reading as fast as I could. We liked taking turns reading from the book of fairy tales. His favorite tale was "East of the Sun and West of the Moon." He liked the girl bravely riding away on the bear, not knowing the bear was really a prince. One day I told Lester that I believed Bear must be his totem.

He stared at me a bit and then said, "I think you might be right."

I was so pleased that he had looked me right in the eye.

Mama smiled at us and said, "I've got chores to do now, so why don't you all work on a play of one of those fairy tales."

"Mama, Lester ain't gonna wanna play a fairy tale," I said.

"Now, Minna, that's not right. Lester *won't* want to play a fairy tale," Mama spoke sternly.

"That just what I said, Mama! He ain't gonna wanna!"

"No, I would say, 'He *won't* want to play,'" scolded Mama.

"That's what I told *you*, Mama!" I said, getting exasperated.

Lester was laughing so hard he had to hold his belly. He finally said, "You're *both* wrong! I *do* want to play!"

I knew right then that Lester and I were meant to be friends.

We both liked to play our own versions of "Jack the Giant Killer," and sometimes I would be Mutzmag the Giant Killer. We'd let Clemmie be the Giant. He liked that. Our favorite, though, was "East of the Sun and West of the Moon," even if I did get mad at him sometimes for laughing when I played the scary ogress.

When the fence and barn were finished, Aunt Nora and Lester brought up two pregnant goats. Mama said we couldn't pay for them, but Aunt Nora said we already had and that she would take any boy kids back, but not until they were weaned. "Otherwise," she said, "these mamas will wail forever, and the mama goats I have might not nurse another's baby."

After a week at our place the older mama, Magnolia, gave birth to two goats in the night, and Papa named the boy kid Willow. Since he would someday go back to Aunt Nora, I tried not to like him too much. Mama named the girl Willamena.

Another week passed by, and Pearl, the other mama, had not given birth yet but was pacing all day long. So I sat with her and sang all the songs I knew, especially the lullaby song Mama sang to Clemmie and me every night. I was expecting it would be an easy birth because I gave Pearl plenty of raspberry leaves, remembering what Aunt Nora had taught me.

When the time came, I called for Mama and Papa, but they couldn't hear me. All I could see were two little hooves sticking out of poor Pearl, but nothing was happening, so I just grabbed them and pulled, and there the baby came!

Pearl licked her all over, but I felt like that kid was mine, too. I named her Sassy, because she liked sniffing the sassafras bush.

Every time I could sneak into the barn and sing to the baby goats, I did. I believe they appreciated it, and I think Sassy thought I was her other mama, sort of like I thought of Aunt Nora as my other mama. Maybe a part of me inside, maybe my heart, remembered that Aunt Nora's was the first face I saw when I came into the world.

When Aunt Nora heard that I had delivered the goat by myself, she congratulated me and said I was a true midwife now, on account of delivering a kid!

Chapter 10

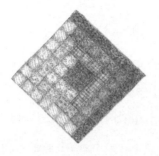

The Secret Trade

One day in June, Mama and Papa let me go into town on market day with Aunt Nora and Lester to sell and buy goods. We helped Aunt Nora and Lester pack their wagon with goat cheese, wool, vegetables, clay pots, and baskets. Mama handed me our basket of vegetables, some of our chickens' eggs, and the Pinwheel quilt.

"Mama, it's boilin' hot out. I won't need this quilt," I started to say. Then I saw her face, and I just knew. "No, Mama, this is Papa's favorite! You can't sell it!"

"Never mind, Minna," said Papa. "You need new boots and a warm winter coat if you're gonna start school this fall."

Mama chimed in. "But first we need more cotton stuffing for my quilts, a sack of rice, beans, salt, and another shovel. The one we have is too small and keeps breaking. Minna, you and Aunt Nora pick out a sturdy one, and *if* there's any money left over, try on some boots and a coat, larger than you need so they'll last two years."

I saw Papa patting the quilt. "There's a good story behind this quilt, but even when the quilt goes, we'll have the story."

"What story, Papa?"

"You don't know?" Papa picked up Clemmie so he could sit on the wagon for a bit with me and stop his whining. "This quilt won top prize at the county fair and was being auctioned off. When I saw the beautiful red-haired gal that made the quilt, I bid all the money I had on it and won! It cost a lot, too!" Papa laughed. "Every suitor around was trying, because if you won, you didn't only win the quilt, you got to dance with the one who made it. And that's how I won your mama!"

Mama smiled at him but quickly turned away and wiped her eyes.

"Mama, there must be another quilt I can try to sell."

She said, "No, the others aren't finished and are already promised. Take it, Minna. It's okay. I can make another. Like Papa said, we have the story." Mama was trying to sound firm, but her voice was shaky.

Aunt Nora patted Mama's shoulder and said, "Marcy, we'll make sure it fetches a high price.

You all go on back now. I have a couple of things left to get ready."

When Mama, Clemmie, and Papa went back up the hill, Aunt Nora told me to follow her into her house. "Now, Minna," she spoke in a low voice, "I don't like secrets unless they are for protection or surprises. Do you understand?"

I nodded but felt a little uneasy.

"Good. We're gonna switch quilts. We'll sell the one your mama gave me, and I'll keep the Pinwheel quilt here."

"Aunt Nora, you'll keep the Pinwheel quilt?" I didn't understand.

"Yes. I'll keep it safe until the right time comes to return it to your mama."

"But, Aunt Nora, we traded. You've given us goats and...you need that quilt," I protested.

"Pfff! Lester and I each have woolen blankets and a bear hide my husband got us." Lester walked

74

in just at that moment. "What's warmer than bear fur, Les?" Aunt Nora asked him.

"Nothin'."

"See? Now, this Log Cabin quilt isn't as fancy as the Pinwheel, and it may be hard to fetch as much money, but we'll try. Do you want to do that?"

I shrugged. "Yes, but…well, it's awful nice of you, Aunt Nora."

She just waved it off and started scolding Lester and me, telling us to hurry up and get into the wagon, that we were holding her up and we wouldn't get a good spot at the market if we kept dallying.

I knew her scolding was only that hard shell of hers trying to protect all that soft stuffing inside. Lester and I just shook our heads, smiling at each other, then raced to the wagon and waited for her.

Chapter 11

An Ugly Secret

When we went down to the marketplace, Mr. Baker, Kevin's father, directed us to a selling spot farthest away.

"But why there, Mr. Baker?" I asked. "We're one of the early ones, and we want a good spot over here." I pointed to where Lottie's and Souci's mothers were setting up. "Some people won't even walk all the way down there. It's too far and hot!" I complained.

He growled back, "Whites sell up here, colored folks over there!"

"But, Mr. Baker—"

"Miss Hopkins, it ain't my fault you're riding with the colored folks. Indians, Negroes, all the same." He grabbed my hand and put it next to Lester's, saying, "If you can't tell dark from light, you got a problem. And it's gonna get worse, you git it?" His face was so close to mine I could smell his bad breath and see his brown teeth from the wad of chewing tobacco he held in his cheek.

Aunt Nora steered the horse to where Mr. Baker had pointed. "That's all right, Minna," she said softly, but there was a bite in her voice. "I always sell over there and have my own loyal customers. This isn't your battle to fight right now."

Lester added, "Besides, Minna, you can walk up and down with the quilt in the white area."

"It just ain't right. We were here early enough," I grumbled. "Mr. Baker thinks he's so important. He acts like he's the sheriff. His boy is the meanest kid around, and now I know how he got that way."

"Nonetheless, it's best you don't make a fuss. Just take your ma's quilt where the white folks are, to get the most for it," Aunt Nora said. "We can sell the eggs and vegetables for you."

"But, Aunt Nora—"

"It's best for *all* of us," said Aunt Nora sharply.

"Yes, ma'am." I looked down and Lester patted my back. I hadn't realized I was shaking a little. Mr. Baker had really frightened me. I was so wishing Papa were here. He would have set Mr. Baker straight.

People, mostly dark skinned, started buying from us as we were still setting up. Aunt Nora showed me how to make change as we sold Mama's vegetables first. Then she said, "Now, Minna, you gotta drive a hard bargain for that quilt. Don't just take your first offer. You show 'em the tight, even stitches. Your mama's quilts are famous, so you let them know that!"

Both Aunt Nora and Lester told me what to say and how to act and how to count the money so I would know if it all added up right. In the end I was so nervous and confused, Lester said, "I'll stand there at the divider line with a basket of eggs, so if you need to know anything, you just say your helper is holding your eggs and you gotta check somethin' first."

Finally I ran off with Mama's quilt in my arms. I walked up and down the street calling out, "Famous Marcy Hopkins Log Cabin quilt for sale! No other like it!" Some people walked by without even a glance my way, and some offered such low prices, I said, "You don't know what you're lookin' at! Can't you see these fine stitches?"

Souci and Lottie were sipping lemonade together, and I ran up to them and said, "Hello there!" Both of their mothers examined the quilt and admired it, and Souci asked, "Minna, where is your ma?"

"She and Papa are at home tending things," I said, staring at Lottie's pretty lace collar. "Lottie, you sure have fine clothes."

"But how did you get here?" pressed Souci, pulling at my arm so that I would look at her instead.

"Oh, I came with Aunt Nora and Lester," I said, pointing to Lester, standing at the divider line with the basket of eggs.

Lottie's lip curled up on one side as she drawled, "Why?"

"I came to sell things," I answered, thinking she no longer looked so pretty making that face.

"But why did you come with *them*?" She was now frowning at me.

"They let me come with *them* because they're my *friends*," I answered.

"A *colored* boy is your friend, Minna?" Lottie asked in disbelief.

He'd be your friend, too, if you only knew him, I was thinking, glancing over at Lester. He must have seen their mean faces, because he looked away.

Kevin Baker and Clyde Bradshaw joined us, and Kevin grunted, "Do you want me to beat him up to show him his place?"

"Yes, Kevin, I think you should, to show him his place," said Lottie, her mouth now creeping into an ugly smile.

"He's *not* my friend," I said quickly. I could hardly believe I had blurted out a lie. "He's just my helper. See, he's holding our basket of eggs, so I can sell my ma's quilt."

"I heard you say you were *friends*," taunted Kevin. "Figures a redheaded witch would be friends with a stick of coal."

The others laughed.

I was so angry that I forgot to be afraid. I looked up at Kevin's face and stood as tall as I could. "Kevin Baker, you don't know anything! Lester is *lots* of things. He's white, too."

"He's a mixed breed, which means he's *nothin'*. But you wouldn't know, 'cause you're so stupid. You don't even go to school. You're just like him." He pointed his thumb at Lester.

Souci's mother chimed in. "Kevin Baker, don't you have better things to do?"

"Yes, ma'am, I do. Come on, Clyde," he huffed, and the two boys walked away, scuffing up clouds of dirt and scowling over at Lester.

Mrs. Smith, Lottie's mother, took the quilt from my arms and said, "Minna, I think my sister in New York would like this quilt. She sells them, you know." She poured coins into my hands so fast I couldn't count them. I hadn't even told her a price, and she didn't ask me, either. She just took the quilt as if it were our bargain.

I ran over to Lester and showed him the money. He began counting it. "Not so bad," he said, "but not so good, either." He could see from my face how rotten I felt. "But it's somethin'," he added. "And somethin' is better than nothin'."

"But it won't buy everything I need," I said, feeling like I wanted to go grab the quilt back.

"Well, look, I sold your eggs, too." He poured more coins into my hands. "Let's go to the general store. Maybe Mr. Hubbard is having a sale."

I hesitated.

Lester asked, "Do you want me to go with you or do you want to go by yourself?"

"I can go by myself. I think your *elisi* needs your help more."

Lester looked a little hurt. "Did those kids tease you about me?" he asked.

I didn't know what to say, so I shrugged.

"Thought so. I'll meet you back at the wagon." He turned and ran off.

I was wishing I hadn't come to town at all, and I wondered why Mama hadn't come with me instead of Aunt Nora. Lately, she never wanted to leave Papa's side, but Papa was getting better. Couldn't she see that?

In the end I had enough for the cotton, rice, beans, and salt, a sturdy shovel, and some second-hand ankle boots, a size too large. There was not enough left for a coat, but just enough left to buy Papa and Lester each a banjo pick and new strings.

Making sure the music wouldn't stop made me feel a little better about not getting a coat, but it was real hard to be cheerful when I climbed into Aunt Nora's wagon. I was feeling like I was never going to get a coat and never going to get to go to school, and people were always going to call me stupid.

But there was a worse feeling in my stomach. I had been teased for being friends with Lester. Had I pretended he wasn't my friend so they would like me, or was I only trying to keep Kevin from beating up Lester? I wasn't sure of the answer, but there was no one I could share this ugly secret with, not even Lester, my only friend.

Chapter 12

Little Folk

As we pulled out of town, we had to pass by Souci and Lottie. They were talking to each other but staring at me. I waved good-bye, but they didn't even lift a hand.

"Who would want to go to school and be *their* friend, anyway?" I grumbled.

Aunt Nora patted my knee, but Lester said,

"If you go to school, you'll turn out just like they did—mean."

"I will *not!*" I burst out.

"Will too."

"Will not!"

Aunt Nora glared at us. After a bit Lester mumbled just loud enough for me to hear but too soft for Aunt Nora's ears, "Will too."

"Will not," I whispered back barely loud enough for even Lester to hear, thinking I had had the last word until I heard the faintest, "Will too."

We kept going on like this until we reached the woods and Aunt Nora began singing a Cherokee song.

"Do you know what the song means?" I whispered to Lester.

He nodded. "She's singing to the little folk in the trees and under rocks. She's asking them to tell the bears and panthers to let us pass by unharmed. In return for the favor she'll put out extra grain and milk for the little folk."

I said, "Do you think the bears and panthers are listening, and they'll eat the gifts instead?"

Lester nodded and we both giggled. I couldn't stop giggling, but it was only because I was so happy our fight was over and we were friends again.

"How do the little folk get along with the bears and panthers?" I asked Aunt Nora. "Don't they get eaten up like rabbits?"

"No, the Yunwi Tsunsdi are friends with everyone and know the language of all the plants and animals. They help the plants grow so the animals have food, and they even store nuts for the squirrels so they can find them in the winter."

Lester asked, "What do the animals do for them?"

Aunt Nora thought about this for a bit, then

turned to Lester, smiling. "They give them rides through the woods. On a full moon sometimes you can hear screeching. Those are the Yunwi Tsunsdi children racing on the backs of bobcats."

"Oh," I said. "I thought that screeching sound was a squirrel getting killed or raccoons fighting."

Aunt Nora ignored me and said, "If a child ever sees one of the little folk, they are not to tell anyone for seven days."

"What will happen?" asked Lester.

"Very bad luck," said Aunt Nora. "Just as it's bad luck to kill a wolf."

"What do the little folk look like?" I asked.

"The Yunwi Tsunsdi? Oh, they are about a foot high and—"

"Whose foot?" I asked.

Aunt Nora looked at me with raised eyebrows. "Maybe *your* foot or maybe smaller," she said, then glanced all about as if she was looking for them. "They wear the old Cherokee clothes, with colorful feathers in their hair. The ladies are very delicate and like to dance. They all speak Cherokee."

I was curious about this, because my grammy had told me they sounded Welsh and wore red caps. I wondered if they all got along or if they fought.

We passed by a waterfall and stopped to let the horses drink and to wade our feet into the cool water. Aunt Nora pointed up to the top of the falls. "Do you see that rainbow where the sun hits the bouncing water?"

"It's beautiful," I said.

"The little folk are playing in that mist."

"Which little folk?" I asked. Aunt Nora looked at me, puzzled. "The Cherokee or the Welsh?"

"Ah," she said, and nodded. "All of them. The colors in the rainbow mixed together make all the brown shades of the little folk. Some are more yellow, some are more pink, some more green, and mixed together, the colors turn to the brown shades of all the people. But when the light and water play together in the air, we see the colors dancing as the circle of the rainbow."

I smiled at Aunt Nora. "I'm glad the little folk all get along with each other." Lester smiled, too, and so did Aunt Nora.

She squeezed my hand and said, "They're smarter than us, Minna. Little folk can teach big folk a few things, if big folk would only listen."

Chapter 13

Come Away

In midsummer I turned eight. I helped Mama and Papa work in the garden, but Papa had to take a lot of breaks because of his cough. He would just say, "Time for a banjo break, Minna. I think being eight is big enough to learn the banjo, and you've got the prettiest voice besides your mama."

And so we would sit on the porch and he would teach me how to play.

At night Papa would ask me to play what I had learned. My first song was this one:

This old man, he played one,
He played knick knack on his thumb;
With a knick knack paddy whack, give a dog a bone,
This old man came rolling home.

"I don't know if I'll ever be able to play like Lester," I said, getting frustrated.

"One step at a time, Minna. If you love what you're doin', that will help you learn it," said Papa. "Love what you do, that's all that matters. The birds of the woods don't worry about who sings best, and Clemmie doesn't mind, either, do you, Clemmie?"

Papa took Clemmie on his lap to play finger games. They acted out the animals and numbers on their hands. In one song Clemmie liked to shout "Noah, Noah" every time the part came when we sang:

"Who built the ark? Noah, Noah!
Who built the ark? Brother Noah built the ark.
Now didn't old Noah build the ark?
Built it out of hickory bark....
Now in come the animals, two by two,
Hippopotamus and kangaroo."

That was Clemmie's favorite tune, but my favorite song of all was Papa's favorite, too: "Come Away."

After we sang "Come Away" and Mama took Clemmie to bed, Papa set his banjo down, and I climbed up on his lap. He said, "You're getting big, Minna."

"Too big for laps?" I asked.

"Not too big for mine," he said softly, "but

too big to still be at home. It's time you went to school."

I could hardly hold back my smiling just thinking about all the friends I would have; but Papa was very sick, and they needed me at home. "Papa, I can't go to school. You and Mama need me here."

Papa just looked at me real steady and said, "They have books and a teacher at school, Minna. You can learn things there that you can't learn at home."

"But I still don't have a coat," I quietly reminded him.

"Minna, don't you worry about a coat. I'll think of something."

But he never got the chance. Papa died at the end of that summer.

Chapter 14

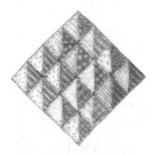

A Fallen Leaf

The wind wanted to come into our little house and sweep me away with it. It wanted me to go up with the wispy smoke from our woodstove and swirl among the leaves in the branches of the trees. And I wanted to be swept up into the air, away. I wanted to be as light as a fallen oak leaf, dancing with the wind, but I could not get out of bed. My heart was a heavy stone in my chest, pressing me toward the earth where they would lay my papa that day.

"Minna," came my mama's voice, tight and high and close to breaking, like the string on Mr. Miller's fiddle.

I moaned and rolled over, burying myself under the Pinwheel quilt Aunt Nora had brought back to us the day before Papa died. Mama sat on the bed, and Clemmie clumsily crawled up on my feet. He was still happy, too little to know what he had lost.

"There are things you can't tell a child," Mama had told me when I asked her if we should tell Clemmie that he would never, ever see Papa again.

I guessed at eight I was a child no more. That thought made the stone in my heart grow heavier.

"Please, Minna." Mama uncovered my head and whispered in my ear. She smoothed away the strands of hair I had let cover my eyes to block out the morning light. "I need your help today. Papa needs your help, too."

I swallowed. It hurt to speak. "Papa's not here," I managed to say.

"Oh, but he is," said Mama. "Can't you feel him? Can't you hear him in that wind? He knows how you love to play in the wind. That's why there's such a burst of it today."

"Papa is the wind!" said Clemmie. "Papa is the wind!"

Right then I knew what my job was going to be, and something took over. I sat up. "That's right, Clemmie," I said. "Papa *is* the wind, and the wind is swirling all around us!" I put my bare feet on the floor, white and ghostlike against the dark wood, and stepped lightly across the room to pull open the door latch. The cool mountain air rushed at me. "Come in, Papa! Come kiss our cheeks!"

Clemmie clung to my nighty with one hand,

and his other little fist rose up in the air. Mama came over and scooped up Clemmie. We all lifted our faces to the sky, letting the wind whip our wet cheeks dry.

At the church we sang "Amazing Grace" for Papa. Clemmie was not feeling comfortable with all the wet eyes and sniffles. He whined and cried out, "Where's Papa? I want Papa!" So when it was my turn to get up and sing what Papa had taught me, I let Clemmie come up, too. He was clinging on to my dress anyway and would have bawled if I had left him on the bench.

Clemmie turned shy facing all the people, but he kept a hold of my dress and mumbled along while I sang:

"'Come away,' sang the river,
To the leaves on a tree,
'Let me take you on a journey,
If the world you would see.'

103

So the leaves, gently falling
From the tree on the shore,
Flowed away on the river
To come home nevermore."

People came up to me afterward and said, "Your papa would be proud."

Mama corrected them saying, "He *is* proud, and so am I."

After the service and the burial, everyone from the church came to our cabin. Each family brought us a basket of food, all kinds of strange goulashes and breads and sweets I might have loved if I had felt hungry, but I didn't care for any of it. I sat on a stool beside the woodstove with Clemmie on my lap so no one would step on us. I couldn't figure out how so many people could squeeze into our little cabin, but somehow they managed it. They all were talking about my papa like they knew him well.

I just couldn't stand it! They all wore black—black like the coal mines that had killed my papa. Papa was done with black. He wanted all the nice bright colors of the day, and if everyone had really known Papa well, they would have known that.

Chapter 15

A Surprise Gift

September came and school started. Mama said I could go, but I still didn't have a coat. There was no use starting something I would have to quit when the weather turned cold. Besides, there was enough to do at home. There were apples and vegetables to pick, corn to husk, lots of canning, cotton to card, goats to milk, chickens to feed, floors to sweep, sticks to collect, but most of all, Clemmie to watch so Mama could sew. I hardly got to see Aunt Nora and Lester.

Two nice things happened, though, after Papa died. The first came two weeks after the funeral when Shane Hunter and his pa knocked on our door.

Mama opened the door and said, "I didn't even hear you coming up the steps."

Shane was carrying a big brown puppy with long ears. "Well," said Mr. Hunter, "if you had this hound, you would know we were coming long before we marched up these rickety steps. I think we need to fix that first one there."

Clemmie and I were jumping to see that puppy, and he was squirming to see us, so Shane put him down on the floor. He just about knocked little Clemmie down, but I scooped the puppy into my lap before Clemmie could even think about crying. The puppy licked our faces, making us giggle.

Mama was saying, "That's a nice offer, Charlie, but we can't take it."

My giggling stopped. "Oh, Mama, *pleeeease*? I'll take care of him."

Mama wiped her hands on her apron and said to Mr. Hunter, "I would like to. I haven't seen Minna laugh in so long, but—"

"Look, Marcy, you won't need to worry about the food for him. I've got that covered. If we kept him, we would be feeding him anyway; but having three is too many, so if you took him, you would be doing us a favor. I'll send down ham bones and scraps, really."

Mama was stroking her forehead, which meant she didn't know what to do, so I just stared up at her, thinking in my head, *Please, please, please, let us keep him*. He felt so warm, like one big ball of love wrapped up in soft fur. We needed him.

"You ought to have a hound to protect your livestock and corn, too," said Mr. Hunter. Then he said in a low voice he wanted only Mama to hear, "He'll soon be big enough to scare off the coons and wildcats. You don't need any more losses, Marcy."

"Please, Mama?" I said in a little voice, but she knew how big I meant it.

The puppy was licking Clemmie's toes, making him laugh his belly laugh.

"I don't think I have a choice," Mama said sharply, but she was smiling. "What's his name?"

I jumped up and hugged Mama. Shane told us, "I've been calling him Squirt because he was the runt of the litter."

"Just like Shane," said Mr. Hunter, laughing. "And he'll grow big like Shane did." Shane was two years older than I was, but a lot bigger.

Clemmie tried to say "Squirt," but it came out "Skirt" no matter how many times I corrected him.

"You can name him somethin' else," said

Shane, squatting down to pat the puppy. I wished then that Shane could be my older brother, and I wished all over again that I could go to school to make friends.

Mama picked up the puppy, looked into his loving eyes, and said, "Okay, Buster, I guess you are part of our family now." So the name Buster stuck.

The goats didn't think very highly of Buster, and Mama said that was because they had a little devil in them. Buster was trying to be the big protector, but they would butt him and mostly hurt his feelings and his pride. The chickens liked him, though, and let him round them up when Clemmie and I tried to get them all back in the barn at night so they would be safe from the wild critters. Rounding them up was a fun game for all of us. I think even the chickens liked it, but that kind of thing isn't as easy to tell with chickens.

Buster wasn't just a dog. Somehow he seemed

to know who felt the gloomiest at any moment,
and would put his head in the sad lap and mag-
ically take away all the bad feelings. It was as if
he wore our sadness on his face. His eyes were so
awfully droopy and sad that we couldn't help but
laugh sometimes.

Clemmie loved Buster as much as I did and would not take a nap or go to sleep unless Buster was cuddling with him. Mama should have kept Buster outside with the goats, but when she saw how happy he made everyone, she let him stay inside, saying, "'Dog' is 'God' spelled backward, so you know there is a lot of God in a dog."

I think Dog was Mama's totem.

Chapter 16

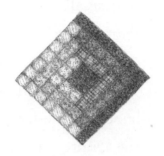

Minna's Mountain

The other nice thing to happen after Papa died was having the Quilting Mothers sew quilts at our cabin with Mama.

They started coming on account of Lottie Smith's rich aunt from New York, who sent Lottie fancy clothes that didn't look like ours. Lottie's dresses had lace and ribbons and flowered patterns, and she had dainty boots with buttons. I always wished I would get her hand-me-downs; but Souci got them, and when she was done with them, they were too small for me. Anyway, Lottie's aunt was buying up quilts from Appalachia and selling them up north for lots more money than they could sell for in our towns. This was a big help to a bunch of the families on Rabbit Ridge and gave the Quilting Mothers a lot more work.

The mothers would come to Mama's house because Clemmie was little and hard to cart around. The other children were in school except for me—and Lester, of course. Sometimes Aunt Nora would come, too, and we would go outside to look at the goats. Every time we did, she would pick some plant or tree and see if I knew about its uses.

"Well, look here at this old pine tree," she said. "I wonder what it can do?"

"Its bark is good for nails and hair and skin… and…" I was trying to think of the other things. Aunt Nora put her hand over her heart and pretended to be in pain.

"It's good for the heart and old-age sicknesses. It makes people live longer!" I blurted out.

Aunt Nora winked at me and fluffed my hair. I think she liked talking to me more than the mothers, even though she knew them well because she had helped them all in childbirth and with sickness.

"Nothing helped my papa, though," I said. I wanted to ask her why the plant medicines didn't work for him. She seemed to know what I was thinking and sat on the porch steps with me and Buster.

"Minna, sometimes we don't have all the answers, but that's okay. We're too small to know everything. Life is a great mystery, and all we can do is try to tell stories to make sense of our time here, and try to make something with the gifts that are given to us."

"I know, I know. Askin' and thankin'," I said, "but I asked and I thanked, and Papa still died." I bit my lip to keep it from quivering.

Aunt Nora put her arm around me. "Sometimes the Great Spirit needs—"

I knew it was rude, but I interrupted her anyway. "I know. The Great Spirit had a bigger purpose for Papa and took him away. But if the Great Spirit's so smart, he or she would have known that Papa was needed more here with us."

Aunt Nora was quiet for a long time, and I wondered if she was thinking the same thing about her husband and her daughter and Lester's dad. She just said softly, "Nothin' ever dies— it only changes. Time may seem long to you, the time your papa is gone, and the time you are here on this great earth. But maybe it's not so long. Do you see how big your goats are over there?"

I looked and nodded.

"How big are they?" she asked. "Show me with your arms."

I stretched my arms out as wide as I could.

"Now look again at Pearl over there, and put your thumb where her feet hit the ground and your fingers where the top of her head is."

I did that, squinting with one eye.

"Now how big is that goat? Show me with your hand."

I showed her. The space was only about an inch. "Well, she's not really this small," I said. "She just looks tiny because she's far away."

"So to you, right now, she is as small as something you could hold in your palm, but if you walked up next to her, you couldn't even lift her, could you?"

"No," I said.

"Well, maybe there's a lot more we'll understand on the other side of this life, and things won't appear the same as what we think we know now. So we might as well love and pray and give thanks for all the beautiful gifts we have and make the most of living while we're here, don't you think?"

"I don't know," I grumbled. "I just know I prayed and prayed and so did a lot of people, and Papa still died. So what's the use in prayin', then?"

"Do you think the Great Spirit, God, is a sheriff who's supposed to go around and stop all the bad things from happening? And do you think he or Mother Earth *cause* bad things to happen?"

"I guess not." I shrugged. "But what are we prayin' for, then?"

Aunt Nora shrugged, too. "Maybe for more love in our hearts."

"Hmm. Maybe." I thought about this awhile. "Maybe that's what God is," I said, "*love*. And I guess you can't blame *love* when things go wrong, can you?"

"Nope," Aunt Nora said, and squeezed me. "We all have our mountains to climb, Minna, and this is your mountain. It's up to you how you're gonna climb it...in the dark with a heavy heart or with love and light."

I nodded and managed a smile. "Do you think Papa can see us now?" I asked.

"I just bet he can."

I hugged her and stayed there awhile as she rocked me a little.

Chapter 17

Quilting Mothers

We went inside to help the Quilting Mothers by carding the cotton and cutting squares and triangles of cloth. They had brought over rags from old clothes too worn for anyone to wear.

Lots of times when they came over, I would pull out a piece of cloth and ask, "Who wore this?" And every time I did, one of the mothers would tell me which child of theirs had owned it. Usually the cloth had a good story, and I loved listening to those stories just like I loved reading the fairy tales and Bible stories in our books. When you really know all about somebody like that, you can't help but want to be that person's friend, and their stories made me want to go to school all the more.

One day the Quilting Mothers were working on a pattern called Joseph's Coat of Many Colors. It was named after a story I knew from the Bible. It was a beautiful pattern, and I just sighed when I looked at it, and said, "That Joseph sure was lucky to have such a coat. I wish I had one like it."

"Why do you say that?" Mrs. Miller, Souci's mother, asked me.

"Because then I could go to school," I said, a little embarrassed that I had mentioned it.

"Well, now, Minna," said Mrs. Miller, "I don't

know that any of us has a spare coat we could hand down to you, but I'm sure we have some scraps to spare. We could piece them together, and you'd have a coat like Joseph's after all." Mrs. Miller looked around the room, and the other mothers nodded.

Mama quickly protested. "You all need those rags for your own quilts. Don't go giving us things you need yourselves."

They paid no attention to Mama. Mrs. Hunter said, "And we could use feed bags for the inside of the coat."

My eyes filled with tears, but I wasn't embarrassed anymore. I said, "I have a feed sack Papa used to carry me in!" I ran and fetched it. "Will this do?"

Yes, it would do just fine, they told me. Then I thought of something important. "But you need to make quilts to *sell*. You can't take time out to quilt a coat."

"First things first," said Mrs. Miller, and they all repeated it. Mama smiled and shook her head, and I saw tears in her eyes, too.

Aunt Nora got up and left without saying a word. No one really noticed, but I did. I was worried that she thought I would stop teaching her and Lester how to read once I got a coat and went to school. Or maybe I would put on airs the way Souci did because she was a schoolgirl and I wasn't.

I ran out the door with Buster and down toward her cabin but met her climbing back up the path with a sack. "Ah, Minna, here you are," she said, handing me the feed sack of wool I had gathered over the past months.

"But, Aunt Nora, this was part of my payment for all you've—"

Aunt Nora held up her strong hand and said, "That coat of yours has got to have wool stuffing. Cotton won't do. This wool will keep you as warm as the sheep are in winter. And you might want to leave in any feathers!" She winked at me.

I hugged her so hard she almost fell backward. I thought of all the stories Aunt Nora had told me while I gathered the wool—stories of the raspberry bush, the sassafras, the pine bark, the strawberry, the possum and rabbit, the mockingbird, and even old crow. All of their healing spirits would be inside my coat.

Chapter 18

Ready to Fly

So on account of the fact that it looked pretty clear that I would have a coat before the first snow fell, I started school the next day. The Quilting Mothers and I decided to keep my coat a secret in order to make it a big surprise for their children when they saw the pieces of their old favorite clothes sewn into it.

On that first day I washed my face and hands until they were pink. Mama had taken Papa's old clothes and made britches, a shirt, and a small shawl for me, and a shirt and a sweater for Clemmie. I wore the britches and shirt under my patched dress because it was chilly that morning. My only other dress didn't have any patches, but the last time I had worn it was at Papa's funeral, and I wouldn't wear it again, not even to church. And I couldn't wear my summer dress because it was also my nighty.

I was trying to button the back of the patched dress by myself when Mama said, "Uh-oh," and came over to me with her sewing basket.

"Minna, hold still. I can't sew this button on when you wiggle like that," Mama said, with her teeth holding the needle and thread in her mouth, which made her voice sound so funny.

"But, Mama, I got the fever again!"

"If you have a fever, you can't go to school,"

Mama teased me, and put her hand over my forehead.

I laughed. "No, Mama, it's the cabin fever. I feel like a cooped-up chicken ready to fly!"

"Chickens don't fly!" squealed Clemmie, running over to me and throwing his arms around my legs. Buster jumped up on me, too, thinking we were all doing our silly dance.

"Now how am I going to sew this button on?" said Mama. "Clemmie, stop, and, Buster, sit like a gentleman!"

Buster obeyed, while Clemmie sulked by the woodstove. I knew he didn't want to be left alone at home—even with Buster and Mama. Who would sing "This Old Man" or play our game of Where Did Li'l Bear Go? I felt bad and wondered if I shouldn't leave him, but I could hear my papa's voice inside my head saying, "You're getting big, Minna. It's time you went to school."

"Mama, I'm scared," I said. "I won't be able to read that good."

"That *well*. You won't be able to read that *well*," she corrected me. Mama was just as smart as her mama and could have been a teacher, too. Papa had told me so. "You'll do fine, Minna. Just be polite. That's what matters most. And until we have your coat finished, you'll just have to wear your shawl and wiggle a lot to keep warm."

"I'm bringing my jump rope!" I said. "Jumping keeps me warmer than wiggling!"

Mama smiled and finished sewing on my button. Then she handed me a lunch sack filled with an apple, cheese, corn bread, and a canteen of water.

"We'll walk you as far as the fork by Miller's Falls." She bundled Clemmie up and carried him because he didn't have shoes.

I looked up at them. My mama had sad eyes—

beautiful, big gray eyes with little lines at the corners from all the days laughing when Papa was with us. Now those lines looked like they had no reason for being there. But her cheeks were still pink and soft. Clemmie's chubby little hand held on to her skinny neck, and his other hand reached out to me. I let him poke my nose, and then I stuck out my tongue, our old game. I gave him my ear to pull, and my tongue went to that side. He laughed.

"Clemmie, I want you to make sure my Fifi doesn't get lonely while I'm gone, promise?"

Clemmie nodded.

"We better get going," said Mama, which stopped the game and made Clemmie cry out.

"Clemmie, you hold on to my lunch sack and watch how I can jump rope downhill." I darted out the door with Buster at my heels. Buster kept getting in the way of the jump rope, and that made Clemmie laugh.

When we reached the edge of the woods, we took the path that led down the mountainside. I loved those woods, especially this day. The whole world was open to me. The leaves crumbled beneath my boots, and I could smell the wood fire from Aunt Nora's cabin.

"Too bad Lester can't come to school. He can read real fast now."

"Maybe someday they'll let him, but I don't know," said Mama quietly.

We walked on, and finally it was time to say good-bye. "Okay," she said. "There's Miller's Falls. You know the rest of the way from here. It's not too long, but I don't like you going alone. Maybe Shane or somebody can meet you next time. I'll talk to his mama."

"It's fine, Mama. I'm big now."

She looked down at me, her eyes teary. "I know, Minna." She bent down and kissed my cheek on one side while Clemmie kissed my other cheek.

I squeezed his tiny feet. They were stuffed way inside Mama's woolly socks.

Too bad he doesn't have shoes. He would like kicking through these leaves, I thought. I walked backward, waving at them, almost afraid to let them out of my sight. A lump came into my throat, so I didn't say good-bye. I hoped Mama couldn't see my watery eyes, but maybe she would think it was the wind making them water.

Buster was confused and didn't know who to follow. "Go on!" I said, then turned around and ran the other way. The only sound of the woods now was the rustling of the leaves beneath my boots, making the birds hush. I wished I wouldn't frighten them. More than that, I wished I could catch the song of the mockingbird, because then I would know I would have good luck on my first day at school.

Soon I saw Souci and Shane up ahead and

called out to them. Shane smiled back at me, but Souci didn't.

"I'm coming to school!" I yelled, out of breath.

"We can see that. It's about time," snapped Souci.

I remembered Papa telling me how Souci didn't like me only because she didn't really know me, but I didn't think that was a good enough reason to be mean to someone.

"What took you so long, anyway? You're gonna have to sit with the first graders, ya know," said Souci, flipping her curls.

I flipped one red braid over my shoulder. "Well, Mama needed my help at home. I hope I won't be with the first graders."

"Don't worry, Minna. You'll catch up real fast," Shane said, and winked at me.

"Hope so," I said softly, and tried to wink back, but it came out as a blinking squint.

Chapter 19

Welcome, Minna

When we got to the school yard, Souci raced up to talk to Lottie and Clyde, and then they all turned around and watched me. I smiled and waved, but they just stared.

Shane said, "They're such babies." I was glad he was still by my side.

The schoolhouse was just one big room with a woodstove in the back and rows of desks and chairs

and a blackboard at the front, where Miss Campbell had her desk. She was writing on the blackboard when I walked in. "Welcome, Minna!" it said.

I was so thankful that Mama had taught me to read, but that didn't seem to matter. Miss Campbell shook my hand and told me to take a seat in the front row with the youngest children.

"But I can read, Miss Campbell," I said, feeling like I was being wrongly punished.

"That's wonderful, Minna. All the same, this is a good seat for you to sit in for a while."

I heard Lottie and Souci snickering behind me. But soon I forgot all about my classmates, because Miss Campbell was such a wonderful teacher and full of stories. She told us all about Pocahontas and how she had changed her name and married an Englishman. I listened closely to every word and wanted to know more.

I interrupted her. "Miss Campbell, why did Pocahontas change her name to Rebecca?"

"Minna, you need to raise your hand when you want to ask a question."

I raised my hand. "Why did she?"

"Well, she had many names, and that was her Bible name."

"But why *Rebecca*? Why did she choose *that* name? Oops, was I supposed to raise my hand again?"

"One time is fine, once you are in a conversation with me. It may be that Pocahontas chose the name herself after learning that Rebecca—who was the mother of Jacob and Esau—was considered 'the mother of two nations' that sometimes fought each other. Pocahontas had done much to help the English settlers, first by saving Captain John Smith and then by bringing food from the Powhatans to the starving English settlers. She also lived with the English and helped keep peace among them all. So, like Rebecca, Pocahontas was a mother of two nations."

I knew that Rebecca was Joseph's grandma. "Did Rebecca help make Joseph's coat of many colors?" I blurted out without thinking, so I shot my hand up again so Miss Campbell wouldn't think I was rude. I wasn't sure how many questions I could have under one hand raising.

"Why does Minna ask so many questions?" asked Clyde.

"Because she's stupid," whispered Lottie, and those who heard her giggled.

I felt Shane tug on my braid, and slowly lowered my hand, then my head. My eyes were stinging, but I didn't want to cry. I wouldn't be able to blame it on the wind.

Miss Campbell addressed the class. "Smart people are those who ask a lot of questions. That's the end of our lessons for today."

I lifted my head and smiled at her, and on that first day I knew I loved Miss Campbell.

After school I told Shane and Souci to go

ahead without me. When everyone had left the classroom to go home, I asked Miss Campbell if I might have an extra book and notebook that nobody was using. I knew there were extras because Kevin Baker had been sent away to work in the factory, where a lot of children went if they didn't work in the coal mines. The lucky ones stayed in school as long as possible.

"Well, Minna, I am only supposed to give out one of each per student. Why would you need more?"

I shrugged and looked at the floor, hoping she didn't think I was greedy.

"Is it for somebody else?" she asked.

I smiled. "Smart people are those who ask a lot of questions," I said.

She laughed. "And sometimes not too many questions. Here, take these, but don't tell me who they are for." She winked and set several books on the desk.

"Thank you, Miss Campbell!" I said, and surprised her with a big hug.

I ran straight to Aunt Nora and Lester's house, making lots of noise to scare the bears who hadn't tucked in yet for the winter. I saw Lester in the yard and shouted, "Lester, look! Look what I have for you!" I neatly arranged the books on the outdoor bench as if they were in a shop.

"For me?" Lester said, his eyes as big as if I had set a whole apple pie in front of him.

"Minna, how did you get these?" He was already opening the pages and stroking them. I just smiled at him.

We sat together on a rock, both admiring the pictures in the Robin Hood book until Aunt Nora came up behind us. "I don't think we better take them, Les," she said with her eyes squinting.

My heart sank. "Why not? Miss Campbell told me to take them."

"Did she know they were for a colored boy?"

"She said she didn't want to know who they were for."

Lester scooped up all the books, held them close to his chest, and ran up the porch steps. Aunt Nora and I followed him into the house.

"Les, you keep these hidden, and Minna, don't tell anyone what you did," said Aunt Nora sharply. All of a sudden I felt very scared. I didn't want to ask what would happen to them or Miss Campbell or me if the wrong person found out what I had done.

The coat was a fun secret to keep, but this one made my stomach hurt.

"No lessons today. You better run on home before your ma gets worried, Minna," scolded Aunt Nora, opening the door to let me out. This wasn't like her.

I ran out the door like Buster when Mama punished him. I didn't want them to see my tears. Soon Lester came running up behind me. "Thanks, Minna. Thank you so much." His eyes where shining. The wind had made them water, and I thought of my papa smiling at Les.

"It was nothin'," I said with a shrug, trying to say it the way I had heard Lester say it to Papa a hundred times.

"You are *somethin'*, Minna," he said, just the

way Papa would have. He ran back and called out from his porch, "And don't you forget it!" I knew then that he must be missing my papa, too, like he missed his own grandpa and mama and papa. In a sad way it made me feel better.

"I won't forget it!" I called back, and waved.

As I walked home, my head felt like an over-stuffed cotton quilt. I was trying to keep it all stitched together, but the questions just kept stuffing their way in...questions I longed to find the answers to. If Pocahontas could be the mother of two nations and bring food to the Englishmen when they were starving, why shouldn't I bring Lester books if he was starving for them?

I looked up through the leaves at the gray sky. We had learned earlier today about how the leaves turn colors in the fall, but now I wondered why the sky turns green-gray before a storm. Why did it seem more gray in the fall than in the summer? Not that I minded a gray sky. I liked the orange, yellow, and green leaves against it. *Does the sky have to be gray for the leaves to glow brighter?* I wondered.

Was I changing like the leaves, glowing brighter against a gray sky? Lots of grown-ups had said I was a brave girl since my papa died, but wasn't I brave before? Was I different now that I had a mountain to climb? And how could I be smart if I asked so many questions that couldn't be answered?

I lifted up my face to the bridge of branches and leaves overhead and felt the crisp wind on my cheeks. It brought smells of fallen leaves to my nose and the comforting smell of wood burning.

Dear Wind, you can bring me sweet smells, but you can't bring my papa back.

Papa, are you really there in the wind?

Chapter 20

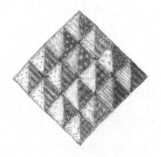

Dark and Light

"Minna! Minna!" came Clemmie's voice from up the path. I saw Mama struggling to hold him. She finally gave up and set him down in his woolly socks. She must have been worrying about me. I forgot to tell her I wanted to stop at Lester's house.

Clemmie started scampering down the path,

but Buster outran him, wiggling and wagging and whining so much you would have thought I had been gone a year! I bent down and let him lick my face. Then I scooped up Clemmie and twirled him around, pressing his soft, fat cheek next to mine. "Mmmm, you smell good. I'm going to eat you up!" I said, nibbling on his cheek like Papa used to do. He giggled. Mama and I took each of his hands and swung him the way she and Papa would, only this time I took Papa's place.

"Mama, what is the wind really made of?"

I was thinking she would say something like "The wind is like love: You can't see it, but you can feel it." But she only said, "Is that what you are learning about in school?" She looked tired, and I could tell she had other things on her mind.

"We are learning a whole lot of things!" That was all I wanted Mama to know, all the good stuff. Her heart couldn't fit in any more of the bad stuff, even if it was something little like how I was laughed at.

"I'm a bad pirate, and only worms and snakes like me!" said Clemmie, kicking up the leaves as we swung him.

Mama looked at me and rolled her eyes, and I knew Clemmie had been a monstrous pirate.

"Worms and snakes like good pirates even better than bad pirates, but sometimes they can't tell the good pirates from the bad pirates until it's too late. Squash! They get stepped on. They have to learn how to tell the difference," I explained.

"How can they do that?" asked Clemmie.

"I'll tell you when we get home." I saw our cabin up ahead with the woodstove puffing out smoke from the chimney pipe. "Clemmie, you and Buster pretend to be panthers and chase me to the house!" I let go of his hand and ran ahead.

Mama called after us, "That might give him you know what!"

She was talking about Clemmie's nightmares. I knew they had been coming every night since Papa died. "That's why *he's* the panther, Mama!" I called back.

"No difference," I heard her say, but without much fight in her.

I let Clemmie catch me at the steps, and we both crawled up to the door like panthers while Buster jumped all over us. When we opened the door, I stood up and looked around at our cabin as if seeing it for the first time.

Now that I was a schoolgirl, our home looked different, a little bit smaller. On one side was the kitchen, and the other was our living room and bedroom combined. The bed Clemmie and I had shared had not been slept in since Papa died. Now Clemmie and his bear and Fifi and I slept with Mama on the big bed, with Buster at our feet.

The outhouse was about as far away from the cabin as I could throw a stone, so when it was real cold and dark outside, we would pee in a bucket inside. We got our water by pumping it from our well. And that was the easy way. Some folks had to fetch their water in buckets from the creek. Still, I was learning that not everyone lived like us. Miss Campbell had shown us pictures of places where some people had plumbing and electricity and heat you could turn on by pressing a button! A few people even owned cars instead of horses. I just couldn't imagine it.

I lit the oil lamp and set Clemmie on a stool next to me while I cut carrots for our stew. Every now and then I pushed a little piece of carrot toward him and said, "This little one likes you and wants to be in your belly."

"Why?" asked Clemmie.

"It wants to help you see better at night." I had learned from Aunt Nora that carrots are good for eyes and skin.

"But why does it like me?" Clemmie had

picked up the little piece of carrot and was looking at it very closely.

"Because you are good," I told him.

"No, I'm a bad pirate," Clemmie said, and
popped the carrot into his mouth.

"Bad pirates are really good pirates who just
forgot about the goodness inside of them," I said,
pushing another piece of carrot over to him.

"Maybe they need more carrots," Clemmie
said, munching.

Mama turned around from stirring the pot
on the woodstove and said in her tired voice,
"Don't eat all the carrots. We need them for the
stew."

"They're turning me into a good pirate,
Mama."

"Well, something better," she mumbled.

"Do you want to hear the song I learned today?"
I asked, trying to make Mama feel happier.

"Yes!" Clemmie said.

153

So I taught him "Great Big House" and the dance steps we learned:

Great big house in New Orleans, forty stories high,
Ev'ry room I been in's filled with pumpkin pie.
Went down to the old mill stream to fetch a pail
*   of water,*
Put one hand around my wife and the other round
*   my daughter.*
Fare thee well, my darling girl, fare thee well,
*   my daughter.*
Fare thee well, my darling girl, with the golden
*   slippers on her.*

The dance steps didn't work the same with just the two of us the way they did when there were eleven of us in a circle, but we had fun anyway. Mama sang along, clapped her hands, and tried to keep Buster from biting at our socks.

After we had finished our supper, I asked Mama how my coat was coming.

"We're still cutting up pieces of cloth and finishing the other quilt. Do you want to go through the bag and pick out some more cloth for when we're ready to sew the pieces together?"

"I want the pieces that have the best stories," I said. "And I need something of Papa's to put in there."

Mama just nodded.

I found his old work jacket, black with soot from the coal mines. For some reason I wanted a piece of that blackened cloth, even though I knew he liked all the nice bright colors of the day. The rest of my coat was going to be filled with those colors: the yellow golds of the birch leaves, the silvery grays and purples of the sky, the deep greens and browns of the pines, the rusty reds of chimney bricks and Lester's pots. Some of the colors were faded, but the faded pieces had been the most loved and had the best stories that went with them. I knew those colors needed some black from Papa's work jacket in there to make them look lighter, just the way the bright leaves in the forest glowed more against the gray sky.

"Mama, do bad things happen so people know what *good* is?" I asked.

"Well, some people say you can't see the light until you know the dark," she answered. "I don't think God makes bad things happen, though. I think there is life and death always, and dark and light, good and bad; but what matters is what we do with it all. It's hard, real hard," Mama said, coming over to me and brushing my hair. "It's hard not to be sad or mad at what happens." She sighed. "But if we can muster up our strength and try to keep loving life itself and each other, then we add a little more lightness to our lives instead of getting buried under more darkness. Does that make sense?"

I nodded, thinking how much she and Aunt Nora were alike in their thoughts. I wondered if Aunt Nora had talked to Mama, too. Clemmie was playing with the cotton on the floor. He looked up. "How can worms tell the good pirates from the bad pirates so they don't get squashed by the bad pirates?"

"They become *glow*worms," I said, and Mama and I both laughed.

"It's time for 'All Through the Night,'" said Mama. She always said that instead of saying "It's time for bed." We couldn't complain about being sung to, especially when the singer was Mama. Her singing that lullaby was like a magic spell being cast over us, and just like Aunt Nora's medicine, it soothed whatever needed soothing, and by the end of it we were usually fast asleep.

Chapter 21

A Sour Sucker

The next morning when I caught up with Souci and Shane, Souci once again didn't even smile or say hello. She just said, "Is that the only dress you got, Minna?"

"Of course not," I said. "My other ones are too pretty for school. I don't want them to get dirty." The lie slipped right out of my mouth, and I felt my face grow hot with shame. Papa would have been so angry with me, and I knew telling a lie was like pulling on a snake's tail. It would turn around and bite back.

"Humph!" Souci snorted. "I bet you're lying." She was carrying a stick and was whacking the tree trunks as she went by. I think she was trying to scare off the bears, but I was wishing then that a bear would take her away. I wouldn't have minded if he were an enchanted prince and she got to live in a castle like in the fairy tale Lester and I liked to read, just as long as she was gone.

"Isn't it the only one you have?" she nagged. "Tell the truth. It's a sin to lie."

"It's a worse sin to be mean," grumbled Shane, looking down and shuffling up as many dead leaves as he could. I hadn't thought he was listening. "Anyway, what's it to you, Souci? All of your clothes are hand-me-downs from Lottie. If you're so upset about Minna having only one dress, why don't you give her some of yours?"

Souci turned beet red and glared at Shane. "Those are *my* dresses, Shane Hunter. Why don't you mind your own business?" She whipped around to me and snapped, "Now look what you've done, Minna, with your lies! Shane and I were friends before *you* came along, and now we're enemies!"

Shane laughed and shook his head. "Souci, your way of thinkin' is like a tangled rope that gets harder to unravel the tighter you pull on it. Just let it be!"

Souci told us she wasn't going to talk to either one of us, so we walked in silence the rest of the way.

As soon as we reached the school yard, Souci spotted Lottie and ran up to her. Lottie was wearing a beautiful dress with lace, one that I knew I would never own, but I sure did admire it. Shane ran off to play with Clyde, leaving me alone staring at Lottie's dress while Souci was whispering in her ear. I was determined to untangle that knot and make friends with them.

"I really like your dress, Lottie," I told her.

Souci blurted out, "It's coming to me next, Minna, so don't even think about trying to make friends with Lottie just so she'll give you her pretty clothes."

"I was just admiring it, that's all!" I snapped back, feeling like the knots on the rope were getting tighter.

Souci nudged Lottie with her elbow. Lottie smiled with her chin lifted and said to me in a sweet voice that sounded like her mother's, "And how many dresses do you have, Minna?"

I glared at Souci and walked away as they laughed.

I decided to be like the rabbit all day so no one would take notice of me and tease me, but now and then at recess someone would come by and

ask, "Minna, when are you gonna wear all those pretty dresses?"

"I have a church dress, but I don't want to wear it anymore," I mumbled, but they didn't care to listen.

I watched Lottie. Everyone circled around her. I wanted to be liked the way she was. I was wishing so hard that she was my friend, because then everyone would be nice to me.

But even though Lottie had lots of friends and I didn't, I still liked school. The best part of the day was the games we played together. We started learning a tongue twister that was so hard at first. But Miss Campbell shocked us with how fast she could say it, so we all wanted to learn how to say it as fast as she could. It went:

Betty Botter bought some butter;
"But," she said, "this butter's bitter;
If I put it in my batter,

It will make my batter bitter,
But a bit of better butter
Will make my batter better."
So she bought a bit of butter,
Better than the bitter butter,
And made her bitter batter better.
So 'twas better Betty Botter
Bought a bit of better butter.

On the way home Shane, Souci, and I practiced trying to say it in rhythm as we walked. I even thought for a minute, when we were all giggling, that maybe Souci had started to like me, but then she blamed me every time she made a mistake. Aunt Nora and Lester met me at the fork. Shane was happy to see them again and was real nice, but Souci just scowled and didn't say anything when they said hello to her.

Once we left them, Aunt Nora said, "That Souci sure is a sour sucker."

"Sure is," I grumbled. "She's made everybody turn on me just because I wear only one dress, while she gets all her pretty dresses from Lottie." I didn't mention that I got caught in a lie. "If I could just get Lottie to like me, then everybody else would, too."

"Doesn't sound like true friendship to me," Aunt Nora said.

"It's just as well I don't go to school," Lester said, walking backward to face me. "Sounds too complicated."

"But I *want friends*," I said, choking on my words.

"Minna, you need first to *be* a friend," Aunt Nora said, and I wondered how I was going to do that when everyone was so mean.

After I taught Lester what I had learned at school, he and Aunt Nora walked me home. I couldn't even try to act cheerful.

Lester finally said, "Minna, school sure has

made you as prickly as a porcupine. You gotta just ignore them. What's the use in having friends like them, anyway?"

I snapped, "Just ignore them like a possum, you mean, and play dead? Lester, you wouldn't know anything about it 'cause you aren't there!"

"And glad of it!" he snapped back.

I felt like crying. I hadn't meant to get into a fight with the only true friend I had.

When we reached my cabin, Aunt Nora said gently, "Minna, why don't you sleep on the problem. The answer might come to you by morning."

I didn't tell Mama anything, except that I was feeling tired. She looked worried and felt my forehead. I went to bed early with Fifi tucked in my arms.

Chapter 22

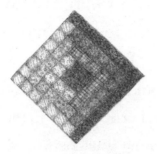

Fare Thee Well, My Darling One

In the morning the answer came. I saw Clemmie playing with Li'l Bear and the wooden lamb. I remembered that when Aunt Nora first told me she was my friend, she said that friends share, and she gave Clemmie and me the little goat and lamb she had made herself. If I was going to win Lottie's friendship, I would have to give her something I'd made, something truly special that I loved. I would have to give her the doll I had made.

I sat in bed and hugged Fifi tight for a long time. I whispered to her that she would have a better home, and I would come visit her as soon as Lottie and I were friends. I told her how lucky she would be to have Lottie as her new mother. Then I cried a little in my pillow.

That morning was crispy cold, so Mama had me wear her shawl over the one she had made me from Papa's sweater. I hid Fifi under it. All the way to school I could imagine the look in Lottie's eyes when I handed Fifi to her. Lottie would know what a good friend I was.

By the time I reached the schoolhouse, I was too shy to give it to her, especially in front of Souci. I decided to place Fifi on Lottie's desk while no one was looking. I wrote quickly on Lottie's slate, "I am Fifi. Please be my new mama."

I darted back to my seat as soon as the others started pouring into the classroom. I didn't dare turn around to look at Lottie.

"Who put this ratty thing on my desk?" I heard the sharp voice come as if it echoed through the canyon. It was a sound I wished would disappear in the gloom. My heart was racing. I heard laughter, and I wanted to turn into a rabbit, go underground, and never come back up. I wanted to be anywhere but at school. I wanted to be anyone but Minna Hopkins.

Clyde read aloud in a high, taunting voice, as if he were a doll, "I am Fifi. Please be my new mama." More laughter. Then came the horrible sight of my poor Fifi flying across the room from one person to the next until Miss Campbell opened the schoolhouse door and Fifi landed, facedown, on the floor in front of her.

Miss Campbell set down the pile of wood she'd carried in, then picked up Fifi and set her gently on a bookshelf by her desk. "What a nice doll. Don't ever let one fall on the floor. Children shouldn't be tossed around, and neither should dolls, especially ones so lovingly made as this one."

I wanted so much to grab Fifi and run home and never come back.

I was so angry at myself. I didn't deserve to be Fifi's mother. At the end of the day I walked out, leaving her there on the bookshelf.

Chapter 23

Clyde's Rag

After school that day I was too ashamed to even stop at Aunt Nora and Lester's. When I got home, the Quilting Mothers were still there, starting to piece the rags together into a coat pattern. I wanted to tell them to stop and that I had decided to quit school, but Mrs. Bradshaw asked, "Now, Minna, which pieces would you like in the front here? Do you like this flannel piece from Clyde's shirt? He used to wear it on fishing trips, but only after his grandpa had taught Clyde how to swim. He even wore it to bed as a nightshirt until it became these rags."

The Quilting Mothers knew I liked hearing the stories about their children, so Mrs. Bradshaw went on, not knowing how much I was hating Clyde at that moment.

"Clyde was afraid of everything after his pa died," said Mrs. Bradshaw softly. "And since his pa got buried under the rocks by the mining accident, Clyde didn't want to go under anything, especially water. Ooh, how he was teased by Kevin Baker, who could swim like a fish when he was three, but Clyde was nearing five. That little boy was the most stubborn thing. It was hotter than Lucifer's den one day, but he sat at the edge of the lake with just his toe in the water. His grandpappy swam up to him on his belly and said, 'I bet you've never ridden on the back of an alligator before, have ya?'

"Clyde said, 'No, sir, and don't want to.'" Mrs. Bradshaw laughed. "It took all day and my poor pappy had the worst sunburn, but he was stubborn, too, and determined to get his grandson in that water. Finally, when Pappy was blowin' bubbles and talkin' underwater, making the silliest noises, Clyde asked Pappy if he was a whale. Pappy said, 'Well, yessir, I suppose I am!' Clyde jumped on poor Pappy's sunburnt back and said, 'Then I'll ride!' And you know, that boy didn't leave the water until he was blue and shiverin'. Pappy gave him his own shirt to wrap in afterward, sayin', 'This is your shirt now, Clyde. You're a man who can swim, and a man who can swim can go fishin' with me.' And that's the story of how Clyde learned not to be afraid of the water," Mrs. Bradshaw finished with tears in her eyes. By that time I'd forgotten she was

talking about the same boy who had taunted Fifi and me.

"I think I'd like that piece to go right here above the pocket," I said, showing Mrs. Bradshaw where I wanted Clyde's rag. "And I'd be much obliged if you could spare another piece or two. One for the sleeve and one in the back."

"I think they would look beautiful there, Minna," said Mrs. Bradshaw.

All the mothers agreed, saying that this was going to be the finest coat anyone had ever seen on Rabbit Ridge, and that it was the best-kept secret they'd known and how they wished they could be there to see their children's faces when they discovered their old treasures sewn in my coat.

Chapter 24

Everybody Makes Mistakes

That night I was worried Mama would ask me where Fifi was, but she didn't seem to notice her missing. After she sang "All Through the Night" and Clemmie was fast asleep, though, Mama stayed by my side, stroking my hair. Finally she whispered, "Are you missing Fifi?"

I nodded and buried my face into the pillow.

My sobs shook my shoulders and the rest of my body, too. Mama patted my back, but it didn't stop the shaking or the tears from bursting out. She rolled me over, lifted me in her arms, and carried me to the rocking chair by the woodstove, then rocked me until I was still.

"I am so awful, Mama. I hate myself," I said, starting to cry all over again.

"Oh, now, that's something you must *never* do." Mama pulled the hair away from my face and wiped my tears with her soft fingers. "You can hate something you did, but you must never hate yourself. I love you, no matter what, and God loves you even more. Everybody makes mistakes, Minna. That's how we learn to be better people and how we learn to understand others when they make mistakes."

She held me for a while, until I finally told her what I had done. At the end I said, "I just want Lottie and the others to like me. I went to school to have friends, 'cause I don't have any!"

"Lester's not a friend?" Mama asked.

"He's a boy, and he's not in school."

"I see," said Mama.

"But I do wish they would be like Lester. I wish they didn't care if I wear only one dress or if I ask Miss Campbell too many questions. Why can't they just like me for the way I am, like Lester does?"

"Lester *is* special, isn't he," Mama said.

"Mm-hmm." I wiped my nose. "But now he probably is mad at me for not stopping by with the lessons. I bet he thinks I've become like the others."

"Maybe you can stop over there early in the morning and make up for it. A friend like Lester deserves your best, don't you think?"

"Yes, and what about the others?"

"I wouldn't worry about the others," said Mama. "I would just go on being Minna. Have fun playing with the younger ones if the others are mean. Sooner or later they'll come around and want a good friend like you."

Chapter 25

Friends Help

The next morning I left home early to give Lester yesterday's lessons. He and Aunt Nora were in the goat pen when I waved from the path. Aunt Nora waved back, but Lester ignored me. I ran into the pen and said, out of breath, "I'm so sorry about yesterday, Lester."

He wouldn't look at me. He shut the goat pen gate and started walking to the house.

"We were worried something happened to you, Minna," Aunt Nora said.

Without turning around, Lester said sourly, "I knew she'd forget about us sooner or later."

"It wasn't that, Lester. I was too upset to come. Something bad did happen...at school, and I felt too awful...too ashamed to talk to anybody."

Lester turned and looked at me curiously.

Aunt Nora said, "Minna, you never need to be too ashamed to talk to us." She put her hand on my shoulder and said, "Go on in with Les. I'll finish up out here."

Lester was still having a hard time with me. He said, "I looked for you in the woods and finally went to your place and saw you through the window with all the mothers."

"I'm sorry, Lester. I was just too sad to come.

I tried to get Lottie to like me by giving her my doll, and…" My voice started shaking. "I thought they would be good friends, like you, but no one at school is like you."

Lester's mouth twisted about, and I saw his cheek poke out from his tongue, which meant he wanted to smile but was trying real hard not to.

"Never give people gifts until you can trust them," he said.

"Yes, I know. I think we better get to the lessons, but I sure wish you could be at school, too."

"If I could, I wouldn't let anybody be mean to you."

This time it was my mouth that puckered and twisted around, trying not to smile. Lester was even more than a friend. He was a big brother.

Because I stayed a little late working with Lester, he walked me to school.

"Aren't you afraid of bears and panthers, Lester?" I asked.

"Nah, I got my slingshot and my knife." He showed me both. Lester and Aunt Nora hunted and were never afraid of the woods.

When we reached the school yard, Miss Campbell was outside, bundling up another stack of firewood. Lester ran up and carried it into the classroom for her, and I carried in a bundle, too.

As we walked in, Lottie looked up and said, "Minna, why did you bring your hired boy to school?"

"He's not my 'hired boy.' He's Lester, my friend," I said, getting all red.

"That's not what you said at the market," Lottie teased.

I saw Lester look at me as if I had betrayed him—the same look Fifi would have given me if she could.

"I said Lester is my helper *and friend*, Lottie! We help each other like friends do, and we're *nice* to each other like friends are."

Clyde laughed and said, "Figures Minna's only friend would be a—"

Miss Campbell had just walked in and interrupted. "Clyde Bradshaw, that's enough! You apologize right now or you'll stay in for recess!"

Clyde mumbled an apology.

"Now, we should all thank both Lester and Minna for helping out with the firewood. I can't seem to keep up with it, and it was so nice of them."

Everyone said, "Thank you," and Lester left quickly but turned and waved to me through the window. I smiled, relieved he didn't believe Lottie.

That day Miss Campbell told us that we each would be given a Sharing Day. It would be a day that we could bring something special from home to share with the class. We would be expected to talk about it. "We learn by sharing a bit of ourselves with one another," said Miss Campbell.

We each chose our day, and I knew what I was going to share.

Chapter 26

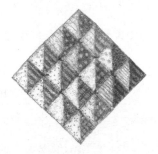

Betrayed

At recess I did what Mama suggested and had fun jumping rope with the younger kids. Sure enough, Lottie and Souci heard us all laughing and having a good time, and they wanted to join in. The younger kids didn't want them to, but I said they could. Lottie and Souci asked me what I was going to bring for Sharing Day.

"One of your pretty dresses, Minna?" Lottie asked sweetly.

"No, something even prettier and more special, but it's a secret," I said.

Lottie started talking to everybody about a "special" doll she was going to share that was given to her by someone "very special." She was looking right at me when she said it and smiled, a real smile that looked pretty. I smiled back and felt so happy. Maybe my plan had worked after all.

When I went back into the classroom, I saw that Fifi was off the bookshelf and tucked in Lottie's bag. When Lottie left school, I could see Fifi's head poking out of the bag, staring back at me. Now I felt my heart breaking. I so wanted to ask Lottie if I could take Fifi back.

Lottie turned and looked at me. She smiled and waved. I smiled and waved back, but my eyes stayed sad.

Souci nudged me and said, "Isn't that doll what

you were going to show on Sharing Day? What do you think Lottie's gonna do with it?" A wicked smirk was on her face, and it took a moment for me to understand that some mean trick was being played on me.

"Isn't Lottie going to show Fifi on her Sharing Day?" I asked.

Souci flipped her hair. "She'll probably throw her in the rubbish heap!"

I stared at Souci, and she just laughed uncomfortably.

Shane called after us, "Hurry up! Aren't you coming?"

"Yep," said Souci. "Minna's just shocked because she gave away the only thing she had for Sharing Day."

"You! You don't know anything, Souci!" I yelled, and ran ahead of them, not stopping until I reached Aunt Nora and Lester coming up the path to meet me.

When I saw Aunt Nora, I ran into her arms and

burst into tears. She wrapped her shawl around me while I blurted out the whole story, ending with, "Lottie's gonna throw Fifi in the rubbish heap, and the raccoons will tear her apart!"

"I know where she lives," said Lester. "I'm gonna go get Fifi back."

"No, Lester, we'll *all* go," Aunt Nora said. "But Minna gave the doll to Lottie, so she will have to think of something else to give her. A bargain is a bargain. You don't take back something you've given freely."

It felt like a long, long walk to Lottie's, and I could not think of anything that I could possibly give her in trade for my Fifi. When we knocked on the door, Mr. Smith, Lottie's papa, answered. "Well, hello, Minna, Aunt Nora, and..."

"Lester," I added, feeling annoyed that he didn't remember. Lester was always helping Aunt Nora give medicine out.

"Yes, I forgot.... Lester."

Just then I spied Lottie peering from behind a door.

"What can we do for you?" asked Mr. Miller.

I was hoping Aunt Nora would explain, but she just nodded at me. I looked down at my shuffling feet and said, "I gave my doll to Lottie, hoping for her friendship, but I would like to have my doll back. I can offer her *my* friendship instead... as trade for the doll." Then I added, looking past Mr. Smith at Lottie, "And I'm a *nice* friend."

"But you already gave me the doll, Minna! You can't take it back!" Lottie snapped, and pursed her lips.

Lester blurted out, "You don't even like the doll. You're just gonna throw her in the garbage for the raccoons to make a nest out of her." Aunt Nora tapped Lester's shoulder to quiet him down.

Mr. Miller looked angry. "Where's the doll, Lottie?"

Lottie ran upstairs and back down. She threw Fifi at my feet, and in a wink I scooped her up and

held her tight. Even a
hurricane couldn't whip
her out of my arms.

"Shame on you, Lot-
tie! Minna has offered
you her friendship, and
that is priceless. You
apologize this minute
and accept her rare gift."

"But, Da, she—"

"Lottie!" he roared.

"I'm sorry and I
accept your friendship,"
Lottie said tartly, and she turned on her heel, ran
upstairs, and slammed a door behind her.

Aunt Nora nodded. "Bargain made. Shall we
go?" She looked at Lester and me and put out
her elbows like a hen fluffing her feathers. We
both hooked our arms into Aunt Nora's and left,
singing all the way back.

Chapter 27

Souci's and Lottie's Rags

The next day I woke up with a cold, so Mama made me stay home from school. I didn't mind, though, because I needed a break from being teased, and I liked hearing the Quilting Mothers' stories and choosing where the scraps were going to go. Hearing the stories also made me think differently about the kids at school.

Mrs. Miller pulled out some scraps of an old woolen coat of Souci's. "Did I tell you this story, Minna?"

"Just a little bit, but not all of it," I said. Part of me wanted to hear it again. I pretended it was a different girl than Souci.

Mrs. Miller laid the scraps on her lap and gave me a piece to hold. "This is the story of Izzy, Souci's cow, when it was just a calf, not much bigger than Buster there." Hearing his name, Buster lifted his sleepy head, but I told him to go back to sleep because the story didn't concern him.

"Well, Izzy was scrawny to begin with, and the poor calf's mother died not long after she gave birth to Izzy. It was bad enough that we had lost our cow, and now it seemed clear that we were going to lose Izzy, too. Souci's pa said he was going to put it out of its misery 'cause it was no use even trying to keep it alive. Oh, that Souci had a conniption fit, and you know she can be feisty with her anger, no doubt."

"Oh boy, she sure can," I said, noticing that Mrs. Miller looked a little embarrassed.

"This time her fits came in handy," said Mrs. Miller. "She begged her pa with everything she had to let her try to keep little Izzy alive. So her pa put up his arms in defeat and told her the calf was hers to take care of, but he was shaking his head.

"Our Souci, who's afraid of the dark, would

sneak out to the barn in the night. Each morning I'd go out there and find her huddled with Izzy under her wool jacket, this one here." Mrs. Miller held up a scrap that still had calf fur on it. "She would have brought Izzy into her own bed if she could have!" The mothers laughed, but I remembered wanting to do the same with my goat, Sassy.

"That cow just grew and grew and ended up giving us the sweetest milk of all!"

Lottie's mother said, "Maybe we all should sleep with our cows to get sweeter milk."

I thought maybe I'd have to pretend I was a calf if I was gonna get Souci to be nice to me. I felt that she couldn't be so bad if she had done all that for Izzy. I chose the spots where I wanted to put the scraps of Souci's old woolen jacket, and the mothers all approved of my decisions. Then Lottie's mom pulled out a beautiful scrap of turquoise velvet.

My eyes grew big and I went to touch it. "It's so soft. What is *this* from?"

"You all know that Lottie had a sister and a brother who were taken by illness and never even reached the age of four," said Mrs. Smith gravely. The other mothers murmured and cast their eyes down.

"Even though Lottie's never been as frail as the other two, I can never be too cautious, and her da thinks I spoil her and protect her too much. He says she's not a porcelain doll that would break. But it's nothing to what my sister in New York does."

"Is that the sister that's buying all the quilts to sell up there?" I asked.

"Yes, my only sister, and she has lots of money and no children. She thinks of Lottie as hers and sends her all those fancy clothes," said Mrs. Smith bitterly. "Oh, I'm grateful, mind you, that Lottie has nice things to wear and all, but you would think my own sister might also send *me* something nice to wear, too. I know she just wants to make me feel smaller than she is, and that's her way. I wish it was me that was giving Lottie all those nice things."

The other mothers nodded in agreement.

"Lottie's doll has nicer clothes than I do," Mrs. Smith complained.

"Oh, by far," Souci's ma blurted out, and then quickly covered her mouth, but the truth had already slipped out before her hand could catch it.

"Well, anyway, this piece here," said Lottie's mother, fingering the soft velvet scrap, "is a piece of a dress Lottie's porcelain doll wore. My sister sent the doll to Lottie for her fifth birthday. Can you believe a doll this fancy and fragile being sent to a child that age?" The other mothers shook their heads. "Well, Lottie wanted to sleep with the doll. Of course, I wouldn't let her. I had her da make a bed for it, its own bed, so that Lottie would have the doll next to her. But do you know what she did?"

"Did she sneak the doll into bed anyway?" I asked.

"Oh, no, Lottie wouldn't dare. Instead she

would take off this dress," Mrs. Smith said, flapping the scrap in the air, "and sleep with it every night against her cheek." She lowered her voice. "Now, Lottie was still in the habit of sucking her thumb, and this soft cloth was what she liked to hold in her hand when she was sucking. The thing became rags, until I had to sneak it away, and I think that's what cured her of thumb sucking!"

I was thinking how lucky Lottie was, but then I thought maybe I was luckier to have Fifi to cuddle with at night instead of a dress. I wondered why her mama didn't make her a soft doll.

"This cloth is so soft I'd like it to be the collar for my coat!" I said, and they all agreed.

It wasn't Lottie's fur collar, but I was going to have a pretty collar after all, and one that I was sure she would admire especially, since it had come from her own doll's dress.

Chapter 28

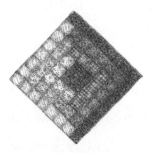

God Speaks Every Language

The next day we didn't have school because it was Saturday, but the Quilting Mothers still came and I was still sick. Aunt Nora came up to bring me some medicines. She stayed a bit to help work on the coat with the other mothers.

"Thank you all for making my wish come

true," I told them. "I'm going to be the luckiest girl in the world."

They seemed glad and Aunt Nora winked at me.

"I just wish Lester was as lucky," I said. Aunt Nora looked down and mumbled something.

The other mothers looked embarrassed. Mrs. Miller said, "It is too bad that there isn't a school for him close by."

"But there is," I said.

Nobody said a word. Finally Shane's mother said, "If it were not for Aunt Nora, my Shane wouldn't even be here, and a lot of us know that both Aunt Nora and Lester have kept us well."

"Why wouldn't Shane be here?" I asked Mrs. Hunter.

She was happy to tell the story and pulled out a very ratty-looking rag. "It was too early for the baby to be born," Mrs. Hunter said, "but I had been working hard—too hard, I guess—and Shane started coming. I sent my Jon up to fetch Aunt Nora in the middle of the night with only a fingernail of a moon to see by. Aunt Nora came with Simon. Simon and Jon…" Mrs. Hunter chuckled, and Aunt Nora gave a flicker of a smile, but it was a sad one.

Mrs. Hunter looked at her kindly and said, "Our husbands played the fiddle and banjo through the night. They said it was to calm me down and to welcome the baby, but I knew better. They grabbed every chance they could to play together…never mind that I was in the next room having a baby and not singing, either." At this Aunt Nora laughed.

"Maybe they were trying to drown out your moans," added Mama.

"Anyway, when Shane came, he was so tiny that Jon could hold him in the palm of his hand. Jon and Simon shook their heads, sure that he wouldn't live but three days. I cried and said, 'I just pray he makes it till morning so we can have him baptized before putting him in the ground.'" Mrs. Hunter gave Aunt Nora another admiring glance and went on, "But Aunt Nora wouldn't listen. She said, 'Nonsense, you keep him warm and loved, and he just may make it.' She gave me herbs that would strengthen my milk and Shane's heart."

"Raspberry leaf, motherwort, fennel, and alfalfa!" I blurted out, and Aunt Nora nodded at me.

"That's impressive, Minna," said Shane's ma. "She also kept me eating chicken soup, which I craved. But Aunt Nora did something else. She held Shane against her heart and sang him Chero-kee songs, quiet like, so Jon wouldn't think she was doing devil magic." Shane's mama glanced nervously at Aunt Nora then, but she was looking out the window with her chin raised high.

Mrs. Hunter continued. "I know God speaks every language, so I didn't mind a bit.

"Simon had given Shane's pa a box of cigars as a gift, and so they emptied it out and put Shane in the little cigar box with this blanket." Mrs. Hunter handed me a scrap of the blanket. I felt how soft it was and put it to my cheek.

"Jon kept the stove stoked day and night for three weeks, and sometimes Aunt Nora came down and even Simon came to help. Of course, when Simon came, he brought his banjo, and he and Jon played music till all hours. Somehow by the grace of God, and with Aunt Nora's help, Shane survived."

"And with all that music, no wonder he's so good at the fiddle!" I said.

"Yes," Mrs. Hunter said, and chuckled. But I

really don't think he'd be here at all without Aunt Nora; so I, for one, would like to do all we can for her grandson. He should be at that school with the rest of our children." The other mothers nodded.

With a mama like Mrs. Hunter, no wonder Shane was so nice, but then, most all of the children on Rabbit Ridge had nice mamas.

Lottie's mother said, "It's all right for us mothers to be talking this way, but the others and our men...they would never have it."

"Have what?" I asked.

"A colored boy learning side by side with white children," Lottie's mother said.

I told them all the story of Pocahontas and how she kept the white settlers from starving and how she was the mother of two nations and also kept the men from fighting just by being kind. I told them how she married a white Englishman and that for her new name she chose Rebecca, after Joseph's grandma, who was also a mother of two nations and probably the one who made Joseph's coat of many colors. I said it all almost in one breath so I wouldn't forget it.

The mothers were quiet for a while, and then Lottie's mother said, "Did you know our family is descended from those settlers that Pocahontas kept alive?" No one said anything.

Aunt Nora was just sewing quietly, not looking up. "I don't want my Lester getting hurt," she said finally. "He's a good boy. That's a nice thought you all have, but he's got plenty to do at home, and I don't want trouble."

"If our men didn't like it, we could all quit our sewing," said Mrs. Hunter.

"No, we can keep the money to ourselves and our children. We can quit our *wifing*," said Mrs. Miller. "Yep, we'll just quit our wifing."

They all murmured things I couldn't hear.

"And they would also lose Aunt Nora, our medicine woman, too," said Mama.

"Can we all stand together and agree on this?" asked Mrs. Smith.

"It may not go smoothly, but what ever does?" Mrs. Hunter asked.

"You all can say this fine, but Lester's not yours. He's all I've got, and he's not even ten yet. I don't want anything happening to him," said Aunt Nora.

"Aunt Nora's right," said Mama. "We need to respect her wishes, but there'd be no harm in us going and talking to Miss Campbell. We'll see what she thinks, and that's all."

I could have told them what Miss Campbell would think. I was excited and scared, but I was also real proud of those mothers.

Chapter 29

The Great Risk

Some of the mothers went and talked to Miss Campbell, and one day she asked me to stay after school.

"Minna, I have to ask you something. Those extra books I gave you, they were for Lester, weren't they?"

"Uh-huh," I said, nodding.

"Would you show me to his house today?"

"Sure I could!" I said. "But I don't know what his grandma will say."

Aunt Nora opened the door before we had the chance to knock.

"I know why you've come, and it's very nice of you, but I have to protect Lester," said Aunt Nora.

"I understand," said Miss Campbell. "I wouldn't ask you to do anything you didn't want to do, but I'm hearing from some of the mothers that they would like to help out Lester, since you have helped them so much."

"Some people may like us, but it only takes one bad seed to spoil the rest." Aunt Nora turned her back to Miss Campbell and put the teakettle on the stove. I was wondering if Miss Campbell thought Aunt Nora was brewing a disappearing potion for her.

Lester came forward with his books. "Ma'am, can I show you what I've done in the workbooks? Minna taught me how to read!"

"Well, my mama did help him some, too," I admitted.

Miss Campbell smiled at me and sat next to Lester. "You did all this? And you just learned to read?" She looked up at Aunt Nora. "He's got a gift for learning. It would be a shame not to give him a chance."

"I don't want him to get hurt or worse," said Aunt Nora, tightening her lips.

"Elisi, let me take the chance," Lester said softly. He stood up and hugged his grandma. He was almost as tall as she was.

"Mrs. Jenkins—"

"Everyone on Rabbit Ridge calls me Aunt Nora, even grown-ups," said Aunt Nora, "so you might as well, too, though I know you're not from these parts."

"Aunt Nora, I would be willing to meet Lester for an hour after school each day if he could chop some wood, rake some leaves, stoke the fire…and be in the class as my helper. If people saw him working, they would not question why he was there. It's a first step and a way for the children to get better acquainted. If it gets uncomfortable, we will quit. I certainly don't want anything bad to happen to you or Lester—or to me, for that matter."

Aunt Nora said, "He's not a hired boy...but I understand what you're trying to do."

"I'd be willing to do all that, Elisi. Please let me," said Lester.

Aunt Nora looked out the window for a bit and then put her wrinkled hand over Miss Campbell's smooth one and tapped it three times.

"Miss Campbell, you're a brave, kind, and well-meaning woman. If you are willing to take this risk, then I suppose we might, too. Let me sleep on it."

Lester hugged his grandma, knowing that meant he'd be going to school. I hugged Miss Campbell and Aunt Nora and tried my best to wink at Lester.

The next day Miss Campbell announced to the class, "You probably all know Lester, Aunt Nora's grandson. He's here helping us out with the woodstove and other chores. It's very kind of him to do this, and I want you all to be polite and thankful."

There were some mumblings and grumblings, but Miss Campbell snapped at the growlers and set them straight.

As the day went on, everything seemed to be going well, until Lottie turned around and said, "Don't you have work to do, boy?"

"Lottie! What did I say?" snapped Miss Campbell.

"You said to be polite and thankful, but he's just sitting and listening to our—"

"I have asked Lester to stay by the woodstove and keep it stoked for us. You are out of line."

"I'm sorry, Miss Campbell," said Lottie.

Lester ignored anyone that teased him. He was

also very friendly, so that helped. I figured since Lester was so good at getting honey from the beehives without getting stung, it was no wonder he could get along with the schoolchildren all right.

Pretty soon everyone was just used to Lester being there in the classroom as the quiet helper. After school he'd stay behind with Miss Campbell, and only the Quilting Mothers and I knew that she was teaching him. I was relieved Miss Campbell had taken over the lessons, too, because Lester was eager to learn more than I could teach him.

It was also nice that Lester and I could study together now. He helped me a lot with my math, and I helped him with his spelling. We tried to outdo each other on "Betty Botter." I think Lester won that one, but it didn't bother me.

What bothered me was the constant worry that someone would find out that Lester was really a student like the rest of us.

Chapter 30

New Partners

On the first Sharing Day, Clyde Bradshaw brought in the watch his grandpa had given him. It had been his grandpa's when he was young, and it still ticked. Clyde went around to each of us, making sure we all heard it. I was smiling to myself thinking about all the stories his ma had told me about their fishing trips and how Clyde had learned to swim. I knew why he loved that watch.

"What are you smiling at, Minna? Is my watch that funny?" Clyde asked, getting all angry for nothing.

"No, I was just thinking about it, that's all," I said. "I bet your grandpappy taught you how to tell time, too."

"Yeah, he did," he said, looking at me curiously. "He taught me a lot of things."

I smiled at him, and I think I saw a tiny curl go up on one side of his mouth, but with Clyde it was always hard to tell a smile from a sneer.

That day after school Souci went home with Lottie, and I noticed Shane was sitting by the oak tree and not walking with me partway as he usually did. He was playing the fiddle instead.

"Aren't you coming, Shane?" I asked. "It's a little cold to be playin' out here, don't ya think?"

"Nah, I'm fine. You go on ahead. I think I'll go in and help Lester clean up."

My heart started racing. The last thing I wanted was for Shane to find out what was going on and then tell his pa, who might tell other pas. I was so worried I spoke fiercely to him.

"Shane! You better come right this minute! Your ma is expecting you at home!"

Shane looked at me, shocked at first, then laughed. "You ain't my ma, Minna, and you must not know her that well. She'll want me to stay."

I was getting all flustered and felt my face go hot. If anything bad happened to Lester or Aunt Nora, it would be all my fault.

Shane could see I was about to cry. "Minna,

what has gotten into you? Are you afraid to walk alone? I'll walk you to your path if you want."

"But then you're gonna come back here, aren't you?" I asked, starting to cry now.

He patted the ground next to him for me to sit down, so I sat. "Now listen, Minna. I know you can keep a secret, right?"

I nodded.

"I know you know why Lester is in there. My ma told me. And I know it's because of you."

I buried my head in my knees. "Please don't tell the others!"

Shane patted my back. "I would never do that! I just want to ask Lester if he'll play music with me on my Sharing Day. Do you think he'll want to?"

I jumped up and put my hand out to Shane. "Let's go see."

When we walked into the schoolroom, both Miss Campbell and Lester looked up, worried.

"Excuse us, Miss Campbell, but Shane has a question for Lester."

I had never seen Shane look bashful before. He was blushing and looking down at his boots. "I was wondering if we could practice some music together," he mumbled.

I could tell Lester was trying not to smile, trying to be tough and big, but his teeth showed anyway. "Sure... sure, that would be fine."

Miss Campbell smiled, too. "Well, Shane, I see you have your fiddle with you. Why don't we break early, Lester, and you boys can go practice. Shane, it's your Sharing Day soon. Will you be playing music?"

Shane looked down at his boots again. "Well, yes, ma'am, and that leads me to my next question. I was wondering if I could share my Sharing Day with Lester—that is, if Lester wants."

This time Lester looked down, and I could see his tongue pushing out his cheek. Miss Campbell glanced at Lester and was quiet for a bit, and then said, "You know, I think that would be fine, yes, very fine. Perhaps you both could also play a tune for us all to dance to."

Both Lester and Shane looked up, grinning, and Lester gathered his things to go. The three of us walked down the path together, and all the while those two talked about the tunes they knew.

I told Lester I was going to come along to ask his grandma something. He nodded, barely listening to me. I was glad they were becoming friends, but I felt a little left out, like I had blended in with the leaves and they had forgotten I was there at all.

Chapter 31

A Masterpiece Every Day

Aunt Nora's eyes widened when Shane came into the cabin with us, but she greeted him like always, made up some tea for everybody, and served us corn bread. Les and Shane gobbled it down and started playing right away. I was so wishing I could be playing the banjo with them, but I wasn't even half as good as they were.

"Almost like listening to my Simon and Jon all over again," said Aunt Nora, and I could see her eyes were a little watery. Aunt Nora and I sang "Turkey in the Straw" and "Polly Put the Kettle On" with them, and her voice grew quieter and quieter, until I noticed that I was singing all by myself. Lester looked over at me and nodded.

I didn't want to go home, but I knew Mama

would be worrying. Then I remembered what I had to ask Aunt Nora. I whispered my question in her ear. She sat there for a long while, and I was wondering if she had even heard me. That was the way with Aunt Nora, though. She never did anything in a rush. She slowly got up, went to a trunk, took out a little bundle, and walked outside with me.

We stood together on the porch as the sunlight was streaking through the dark, lacey branches. "Just look at that," she said. "A masterpiece every day." She clapped her hands at the performance, and I joined her. The sky was apricot and crimson behind the black branches, and the layers upon layers of pale blue mountains in the mist beyond were as beautiful a sight as there ever was.

"Sometimes we forget to look at all the wonder around us every day, but it's always there. That's the biggest secret my *elisi* told me. No matter how bad or mad we are, or even how grand we feel, it doesn't stop the show of *wonder*," Aunt Nora said, gazing at the sight. "It's there, just waiting for us to notice and say, 'Hey, stop your silly thoughts. If you look at me, you will be happy. I'm bigger than all of your comin's and goin's and all of your doin's. I was here before you, and I'll be here after you, so you best pay attention and enjoy *me*, Mother Earth, while you are here visiting.'"

She patted my knee and opened her leather bundle. There was an assortment of odd things inside: stones, feathers, animal teeth, hair, and a piece of denim cloth. She ripped off a piece of the cloth and handed it to me.

"This is from the shirt that my Simon, Lester's grandpa, wore when he and Lester last played music together."

I held the cloth to my chest and couldn't speak. I whispered, "Are you sure? Are you sure Lester won't mind?"

"It was Lester's idea, but he was too shy to give it to you himself. We've got the other half here. I'll let him know. Now you better run along home." She stood and walked to the goat pen without looking back at me.

Chapter 32

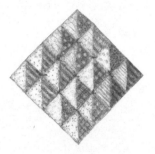

Izzy's Cheese

The weather grew colder and colder, and everyone was wearing coats. I went to school wearing as many layers as Mama could find. One morning she wanted me to wear her big, thick sweater, but I knew she needed it.

"Mama, this is way too big for me, and I won't be able to jump rope wearin' this gigantic thing!"

I threw it onto the bed and ran out the door to meet up with Lester before Mama could argue and even before kissing Clemmie good-bye.

That day was Souci's Sharing Day. She brought some cheese she had made from her cow, the one she had raised herself. Souci told us all about cheese just like she was an expert.

"The making of cheese goes back four thousand years," said Souci. "People think that maybe an Arabian traveler discovered how to make it by mistake. He was probably traveling through the desert and had milk in a container made from the stomach lining of an animal. So the rennet—that's the stomach lining—along with the warmed-up milk made the milk curdle and taste good!"

"Cottage cheese!" yelled Clyde.

"Children, isn't it interesting how wonderful discoveries can be made by mistake or happenstance?" asked Miss Campbell. I could tell she liked the way Souci was teaching us on her Sharing Day, and I began to worry about my Sharing Day. I wasn't going to have anything to teach, or be able to share anything good to eat.

"Now, how did the rest of the world discover how to make cheese?" Miss Campbell asked Souci. I think Miss Campbell had helped Souci prepare the report.

Souci looked at her notes and read, "People think travelers from Asia brought the art of cheese making to the Romans, who must have brought cheese up to England, and then the English pilgrims brought cheese over on the *Mayflower* ship to America." Souci smiled at Miss Campbell, and Miss Campbell smiled back. I was wondering if Miss Campbell would smile like that at me on my Sharing Day.

Souci went on to tell us how she had made the cheese by separating the fats from the solids. "You can use vinegar, lemon juice, or rennet to do this," she said, but she didn't tell us what she used. "Then you heat it, salt it, and let it age in the cellar for two or three months."

She had brought in a round cake of cheese and cut slices for everyone. We crowded around the table, complimenting her on the cheese and how smart she was. I liked our own goat cheese better, but I didn't say anything. I was remembering the story Souci's mama had told me about Souci's cow, Izzy, when it was just a scrawny calf.

I said to Souci, "This cheese is very sweet. I bet it came from Izzy."

She looked at me, puzzled, and asked, "Did I tell you her name?"

I just smiled.

When we went out to recess, Souci asked me why I didn't wear a coat. I told her I couldn't jump rope as well wearing a coat. Jumping a lot was keeping me warm, and I was fast becoming the best rope jumper in the school; at least the younger kids said so. My favorite rope tune was this:

Not last night but the night before
Twenty-four robbers came knocking at my door.

That night when Mama looked sad, I told her things could be worse. We could have twenty-four robbers knocking at our door.

She said, "Now, what on earth would they want from *us*, Minna?"

"Oh, Mama, they would want my coat, first thing," I said.

She laughed then, but I was most serious. My coat was looking so beautiful. The Quilting Mothers were making it into a crazy-quilt pattern because there were so many different sizes and colors of scraps. It wouldn't do to make it any other pattern. And I think they each also wanted the chance to use their fancy embellishment stitches, which crazy quilts are famous for. But I hoped that wouldn't slow them down too much. I was starting to worry that they might not finish it for my Sharing Day!

Chapter 33

The Fragile Doll

On her Sharing Day, Lottie showed us the porcelain doll her aunt from New York had sent her. We all thought it was the most beautiful thing ever and wanted to touch it, but Lottie wouldn't let anyone near her doll. She said, "Nope, it's mine," which made everybody mad. Nobody would talk to her at recess.

I saw Lottie all by herself, sitting against the big oak tree. As I walked up closer to her, I saw that she was crying. I was remembering Lottie's ma telling us how she was always afraid of something happening to Lottie, as if Lottie were as frail as her other children that died or as fragile as the porcelain doll she wasn't allowed to sleep with.

"Lottie?" I said softly, and tapped her shoulder.

She looked at me and turned her tearstained face away. "What do *you* want?" she snapped.

"Nothing. I'm just here to be your friend, like I promised. I bet you were afraid of your doll breaking, and I was wondering what her name is."

Lottie sat up a little straighter and sniffed. "Her name is Mimi."

. "Mimi? That's a little like Fifi," I said.

She nodded. "I thought so, too. I suppose you're showing Fifi on your Sharing Day?" she asked.

"No, I have something else."

"Well, what is it?" she asked impatiently.

"It's a surprise, but it's something you'll really like," I said.

"I liked Fifi," said Lottie, wiping her nose. "I really did."

"You did?" I wasn't sure if Lottie was tricking

234

me again, but she nodded and her eyes were big and honest looking. I sat down next to her.

"I was going to sleep with her, too," Lottie said.

"Oh," I said, surprised and beginning to feel bad. "Maybe I can teach you how to make a Fifi of your own. Would you like that?" I felt my heart leap with happiness as Lottie nodded and even smiled, but just then Souci ran over and grabbed Lottie's hand.

"Come on, Lottie, let's jump rope." Without another word Lottie ran off with Souci.

I went to jump rope with the younger ones to keep warm. And I wanted to keep myself from thinking about Lottie and Souci.

Chapter 34

Just Like Cinderella

When I reached home, the Quilting Mothers were just packing up to leave. I looked at them a little worried and said, "My Sharing Day is tomorrow." I was too afraid to ask if they had finished my coat, especially since they all looked so tired.

"Don't you worry," said Lottie's mother. "Your coat will be ready. All that needs to be done is the collar, and your mama is going to sew that on tonight."

I jumped up and down, ran to my coat, and hugged it.

Mrs. Hunter said, "Well, aren't you going to try it on?"

Once it was on, I twirled around, imagining I was Cinderella going to the ball. As I thanked them, I pointed to each of their children's piece of my patchwork coat, which pleased them.

Mrs. Hunter said, "Well, we sure made it big enough for you to wear for years."

"Oh, I'm going to wear it forever!" I told her.

Mama nodded. "Now I'll just have to get busy and make you new mittens and a hat out of Papa's old woolens."

"First things first, Mama. My coat will keep me warm enough."

That night I kept asking Mama if I could help her sew on the collar. She said she was too busy with this and that and made me go to sleep early. I was so worried she wouldn't finish it.

The next morning I woke up, and the first thing I saw was my coat sitting on the rocking chair, ready for me. The turquoise velvet collar from Lottie's doll's dress was attached, but something else had been added: Trimming the velvet collar was beautiful hand-knotted *lace*! "Mama! Wherever did you get this beautiful lace?"

"Grammy made it. It's from the trim she made for her own wedding dress, which became *my* wedding dress. She and I both agreed to put it on your coat. She wrote to me and said that she will teach you how to make lace so that someday you can add it to your wedding dress."

"Oh my. Did she ever teach *you* to make lace, Mama?" I asked, thinking this would be the finest magic trick to know.

"Yes, but I never had the time and can't remember how. Hurry up now. You can't be late for your Sharing Day."

After I gulped down some corn bread, I went to Lester's house to meet him. He and Aunt Nora smiled when they saw what I was wearing.

"My, my, but that's a warm-looking coat," Aunt Nora said.

I hugged her and whispered in her ear, "But no one can see what's making it so warm!" I wasn't thinking of just that wool stuffing inside, either.

As Lester and I walked down the mountainside, I went over all the stories from each patch of cloth in my head, not wanting to forget any of what the Quilting Mothers had told me.

"You sure did choose the most worn-out pieces, Minna," said Lester.

"That's because the best stories go with them. Now hush, Lester, can't you see I'm concentrating?"

"No, not really. I see Shane up there. I'm gonna

run ahead. He's helping me with my chores, so I don't want to be late, okay?"

"Okay," I said, looking down at my coat. I was still looking down and mumbling the stories to myself when I walked into the school yard, not watching where I was going. I bumped into Clyde.

"Hey, Patches!" he said, and all the others laughed. "What in the devil are you wearing, Minna? Rags and patches, patches and rags! You are the patchiest patchwork girl I've *ever* seen!"

Before I knew it, Souci, Lottie, and Clyde were dancing around me singing, "Patchwork girl, patchwork girl! Minna made of patches, patches of rags!"

Lottie said, "Look, it's even dirty with soot!" And she poked her finger into my papa's cloth.

Then Souci said, "Minna, you were better off with *no* coat than with that old, ragged thing."

I felt all the blood rush up to my face. If I had

been a volcano, I would have erupted. At first I was too stunned to speak, but then I yelled, "Maybe you're right! If I had no coat, then I never would have come to school!"

I broke through their circle and ran away from them, far into the woods.

I found an old log and sat on it for a long time, too angry to cry. I just stared across the fields Papa used to gaze at.

"Oh, Papa, I wish you were here," I said, and then I couldn't help but cry.

I cried for Papa, and I cried for the Quilting Mothers, who had wasted their time. I was crying so hard I rocked that old log.

Then all at once I stopped because I felt something warm and familiar. The feed bag inside my coat made me feel like Papa's arms were around me again. I could almost hear him say, "Minna, people only need people, and nothin' else. Don't you forget that."

I jumped off the log, wiped the tears from my cheeks, and brushed the leaves off my coat. "No, Papa, you were *wrong*. People only need *nice* people. If people can't be nice, then who needs 'em! Sorry, Papa, I ain't going back to school, and I don't care if I never get smart. Smart people have too many troubles and are mean. I hate them!"

I got up, feeling strong and proud, but I didn't feel good.

Chapter 35

Show Me the Way

Facing Mama was going to be a problem. She might not be mad at me, but she might cry, and that would be worse. So I headed up to Aunt Nora's.

The air was strangely still as I walked, then I heard something crunching through the leaves a ways behind me. I stopped to look, but the noise was coming from the other side of the ridge, where

I couldn't see. I knew the bears had gone to bed for the winter. I thought maybe it was a bobcat, or worse, a hungry panther.

Oh, Lord, I thought, *please don't let me die. I'm sorry I said those things. I don't really hate anybody. Just show me the way out of this.*

I stumbled over a rock and took that as a clue. I scooped it up and put it in my coat pocket. Mama had added that pocket because, she said, "you never know what treasures you'll find."

Mama, I may never see you again. At least you won't know how I was teased about my coat, but it will be all bloody, just like Joseph's coat. That thought really scared me, and the noise was catching up.

I grabbed the nearest pine tree branch and scrambled up that tree as quick as I could. My heart was thumping so fast, and I could see my breath coming out my mouth like big puffs from a locomotive train. All the while I was thinking it was useless for me to be climbing, because the

245

panther was a better climber than I could ever be. I was more like the rabbit and shouldn't have had such a colorful coat. I could have blended into the leaves, and no one would have noticed me, no Clyde, no Lottie, no Souci, and no panther!

I perched on a branch, crunching up in a ball, and took the rock out of my pocket, ready to pound that panther in the head when it got close.

The noise stopped, right at the base of my tree. It was hard to see through the pine needles, but I could just make out a dark shape...a dark shape that was climbing up after me. I closed my eyes.

Oh, dear God...oh, Great Spirit, Mother Earth, Holy Mother...little folk of the forest...Papa...help me!

I opened my eyes, clutched my rock, raised my arm, and looked right down into the face of... Lester!

"Minna, what the heck are you doing up there?"

I breathed out, not realizing I had been holding my breath.

"Lester!" I growled at him. "You scared the wits out of me! Don't ever do that again! I thought you were a panther!"

Lester just started laughing.

"It's not funny!" I shouted. Normally, I would have laughed, too, but my feelings were so ragged that they just spilled into buckets of tears; well, it felt like buckets, anyway.

"Aw, Minna, don't cry." Lester looked away from me because he was a polite boy. "Come on down."

"I can't," I said between sobs.

"Why not?"

"You're in the way!"

He laughed again and jumped down.

When I reached the ground, my legs were shaking so hard. Something about seeing Lester's concerned face made me realize how funny it all was.

"Lester, I thought you were a *panther!*" We both laughed. I was laughing so hard, tears started running down my cheeks again. I was crying and laughing all at once.

"Come on," said Lester finally. "We better get back to school."

I shook my head. "Nah, I'm going to your *elisi*'s house. She'll understand why I ain't going back."

"Minna, I thought your mama said not to say 'ain't,' especially since you're a schoolgirl now."

"I *ain't* a schoolgirl no more," I said, walking in the direction of Aunt Nora's.

"*Any*more," corrected Lester as he followed me. Snow flurries were coming down, and we tried to catch them with our tongues and make up what they tasted like.

"Cherry," I said.

Lester said, "Peppermint." Then he said, "Those kids sure can be mean, though, can't they?"

"You saw what they were doing?" I asked.

"Yep. I can see why you never want to go back."

"That's right," I said. "I can make my own

way—people don't always need people. I can choose who I want to be with."

"Yep. With friends like that, who needs enemies?" added Lester. I was glad he was seeing things my way.

I had figured he would, but then he baffled me by saying, "Yep, your pa told me I was *somethin'*, and that it didn't matter if people said I was nothin'. It didn't matter what they did. If I think the right things and do the right things, then I *am* somethin'. You just gotta like yourself enough to listen to your own voice, because that's the *true* voice."

"My pa said that to you?" I asked.

Lester said, "Well, most of it. Some I learned from Elisi and my own ma and pa."

"Lester?" I asked softly. "How did your ma and pa die?"

He stopped walking and looked down. The white flakes were melting as soon as they hit the brown leaves.

"It was a fire," he murmured so quietly I could barely hear him. "Our apartment caught on fire in the middle of the night. Someone grabbed me and carried me out, but it was too late for my ma and pa. I think—I hope—they died in their sleep."

I shook my head, feeling sick. "That's so awful. Did white people start it?"

"Folks said so, but no one could prove anything."

"Didn't that make you hate all the whites, Lester?"

"People are the same everywhere. Some are nice and some are mean, and it hasn't anything to do with their color or where they're from. Some of the Cherokees had colored slaves, too, Minna, and it was a white man who risked his life to save me. I'm a mix of all of them, so how can I hate anyone because of their color? I'd be hating myself. What Elisi says is that you can't help what others do, you only have power over what *you* do and how *you* think. So it's like I was sayin', don't let anybody else's bad behavior change yours."

I thought about that a bit and said, "Lester, I do believe you got the right way of thinkin'." I hooked his elbow in mine, turned us around, and headed back to school.

As we got close to the school yard, I said, "Lester, I should tell them that a panther chased me up a tree, but when he climbed up close and saw my beautiful coat, he said, 'Minna, with a coat like that you must be *somethin'*, so I'm not gonna eat you up today. I'm gonna let you go back to school to tell them how this coat is filled with *somethin'*, but if you come back here thinking you're *nothin'*, then I'm gonna eat you up.'"

Lester laughed. "Yep, you got it right. Maybe Panther is your totem now."

I said, "Well, I'd still like to be friends with Rabbit, too."

Chapter 36

My Coat Is Full of Stories

When we walked into the schoolroom, Miss Campbell looked surprised. "Why, Minna," she said, "I was told you ran home sick. I sent Lester to look for you."

Lottie jumped up, her face all red. "That's not true, Miss Campbell," she blurted out. "We lied to you. Minna left because we made fun of her old coat."

"I'll tell her, Lottie," I said. "It's not an *old* coat. It's a *new* coat."

"But it's just a bunch of old rags," said Souci.

"It is *not* just a bunch of old rags!" I said. "My coat is full of stories, stories about everybody here!"

They all looked around, real puzzled.

"Don't you even see that these are all *your* rags?" They still seemed confused.

So I showed them. "Look, Shane, here is the blanket they wrapped you in the night you were born. Nobody thought you would live but three days because you were so small. But Lester's grandma had them wrap you up tight in that blanket, and they put you in a little cigar box by the woodstove. And your papa and Lester's grandpa kept the fire going day and night for three weeks.

Of course, you lived all right," I added, looking up at Shane. "And you hung on to that blanket for years, until it was nothing but shreds."

"My blanket," he whispered. "I *never* thought I'd see it again." He came over to me and looked at his old rag like he wanted to touch it. The others crowded around me, too, and discovered their old favorite things. They each wanted their story told, and I remembered every one.

I told the littlest ones their stories next. Then I showed Clyde his rag from the shirt he always wore when he went fishing with his grandpa. For Souci I showed the scrap of the woolen jacket she had let Izzy wear when she was trying to keep her alive. And I showed Lottie's rag of her doll's faded velvet dress that she had slept with. I could tell she was admiring the lace, so I whispered to her that my grandma had made it. For some reason I wanted that to be our secret.

"And Lester's piece…" I began. Lester looked up from the back of the room, surprised. Miss Campbell told him to come forward. Clyde was clicking his tongue in disgust. I ignored him and said, "This is a piece from your grandpa's shirt he wore when he last taught you the banjo, right before he was killed in the same mining accident that also killed Clyde's pa."

Everyone grew quiet. Lester looked at the cloth and nodded. Clyde came forward and examined it closely, turned around, and nodded at Lester.

Souci said, "Minna, I sure am sorry we ever said anything bad about your coat."

"Me too," I heard the others murmur.

"I wouldn't blame you if you didn't let us touch it," Lottie said.

"I wouldn't blame you if you didn't want to be our friend at all," said Clyde.

"Friends share," I said, and I let them each

touch their rag. Clyde even asked Lester if he could touch his rag. Lester said that would be fine with him.

Then they asked me where my cloth was and if I had a story. I stood there and turned red. All this time I had been thinking about them and their stories. I didn't want to talk about my papa's miner's jacket because I was afraid it would make me cry, but I didn't know what other story I would have to tell.

I began to panic. I didn't have a story. How were they going to want to be my friends if I didn't have a story of my own to share? Maybe that had been the problem all along.

Lester could see I was troubled and whispered in my ear, "What's on the *inside* of the coat?" I looked at him and smiled. It was almost as if Papa were speaking right through him to me.

I showed them my feed sack inside the coat and told them how it made me feel my papa's arms again. I told them how much I had had cabin fever and had wanted to get out of the house to go to church so I could see them all, and how Papa had carried me to church in that same feed sack before I had a coat. I told them how much I had wanted to come to school to have friends, and how Papa had been trying to figure out how to get me a coat so I could, but he had died before figuring it out.

Phew. I had said it all without crying.

Then I told them how their mothers had come to the house to quilt and had decided to patch together a coat of their children's favorite old things for me. I had chosen the rags that had the best stories, and because the stories were so special, we had decided to keep the whole thing a surprise.

"So, I guess my piece is the feed sack inside the coat. It's the piece that holds all the other pieces around me. It's the piece you can't see, but I can feel it," I said. "And there's wool stuffing on the inside of my coat...." I stopped, thinking of all the stories of the animals and plants, and how Aunt Nora had told me we were all one spirit. For now, that was our private story, which I wasn't ready to share. Instead I said, "Papa told me I'd have a coat with soft stuffing inside, and I told him I wanted it to have lots of colors so everyone would have something to like."

Shane put his hand on my shoulder and said, "Minna, I bet you got the warmest coat in school."

"Well, it took a whole lot of people to make it warm," I told him.

Clyde chimed in, saying, "It better be warm. She's got patches of everybody here all over her! She's the patchwork girl!"

"That's right. I *am* the patchwork girl!" I said, thinking how ashamed a body can be of being called something one minute and then be proud of it the next. This time I laughed, too, and at that moment I didn't think I would ever be cold or unhappy again. I was at the top of my mountain.

Miss Campbell let us out early on account of the snow. Souci went home with Lottie, and Shane walked partway with Lester and me. Their Sharing Day was coming up. Snow flurries were dancing around us, dusting our heads like baking flour. Shane kicked through the leaves and snow and said, "That was the best Sharing Day ever! I'll never forget it."

"Aw, yours and Lester's will be the best."

"Hey, Minna," said Shane, "would you want to sing with us? Maybe you could sing "Turkey in the Straw" and "Polly Put the Kettle On," right, Les?"

"Sure, she could," said Lester. "Let's practice tomorrow. And you know, Minna, you can't let your pa's banjo go to waste. I could teach you everything I know."

"That would be a whole lot!" I said, bursting inside.

When Lester and I reached the path that went down to his house, we looked at each other and he said, "You're *somethin'*."

"*You're* somethin'," I said right back.

"And don't you forget it!" we both said at the same time, and laughed. Then I did something I thought I'd never do. I hugged a boy, real quick like, then turned and ran up the path to my cabin.

A lone and beautiful trill echoed through the woods, and I had to stop and listen. *Could it be?* I wondered. Yes, I was certain. It was the mocking-bird, and he was singing his *own* song.

I was blessed. He must have known I had his feather inside my coat.

Chapter 37

All Through the Night

That night we were all snuggled in bed, Clemmie falling asleep on one side of me, Mama on the other, Fifi in my arms, and Buster at our feet. The wind was whistling outside, shaking our windows, and I whispered to Mama, "It's kind of funny."

"What's funny, Minna?"

"Well, Papa told me that I could learn things at school that I couldn't learn at home, and it's true. I've learned the story of Pocahontas, and I've learned about the leaves turning color in the fall, and I'm better with my spelling and numbers and all, but it was at home that I learned the stories the Quilting Mothers told me about their children. Those were the most important lessons. I might not have wanted to be their friend if I hadn't learned all of their stories. When I have children, I'm gonna—"

"*Going to*," Mama gently corrected me.

"I'm *going to* teach my children that people need to learn each other's stories, like the stories Aunt Nora tells about her *elisi*, and the stories about the plants and animals. And you know, Mama, it was no wonder the others didn't like me the way I liked them. I knew all about *them*, but they didn't know *my* story. And it was the same with Lester. The world is just like my coat. We might all be different patterns and colors on the outside, but really on the inside we all have the same warm stuffing."

Mama stroked my hair. "That's true. We need to know each other's stories so we'll know that on the inside we're all made up of dreams and fears and the same hope to be loved. If we all knew that, then we might know how to get along better. I think that's what your papa meant when he said, 'People only need people.'"

"Mama, I think you've got the right way of thinkin'."

Mama laughed and kissed my cheek. I smiled in the dark, knowing that Papa was smiling, too.

"Mama? I think all that racket the wind is making out there is Papa laughing."

"Yes, that's something he would do," Mama whispered. "Hush now, it's time for 'All Through the Night.'

"Sleep, my child, and peace attend thee,
All through the night.
Guardian angels God will send thee,
All through the night.
Soft the drowsy hours are creeping,
Hill and vale in slumber sleeping,
I my loving vigil keeping,
All through the night.

"While the moon her watch is keeping
All through the night,
While the weary world is sleeping
All through the night,
O'er thy spirit gently stealing,
Visions of delight revealing,
Breathes a pure and holy feeling
All through the night.

"Love, to thee my thoughts are turning,
All through the night.

All for thee my heart is yearning,
All through the night.
Though sad fate our lives may sever,
Parting will not last forever,
There's a hope that leaves me never,
All through the night."

To the Reader

Writers are often advised, "Write what you know," but I would first advise people to write what they *love*. After all, I can't *know* what it was like to be an eight-year-old girl living in a log cabin in the Appalachian Mountains in 1908. But I love this time period, this setting, and Appalachian culture, and I *can* know and share many of the same feelings as that eight-year-old girl because they come from similar experiences in my own life.

I spent part of every summer of my childhood at my grandparents' home in West Virginia. I will never forget the scent in the air, the sound of the cicadas, the misty views of the rolling hills, and visiting my grandmother's friend who lived in a log cabin with handmade baskets hanging from the beams. Nor will I forget the awe I had for Chuck, the handyman of the neighborhood, who once worked in the fearsome coal mines that took so many lives.

Other memories of my childhood in different parts of the country found their way into the story, too, like trying to earn a girl's friendship by sacrificing a beloved doll, being teased about the bold and modern clothes that my mother used to sew for my sister and me, and spending the summer with my brother at our aunt and uncle's farm in Kalispell, Montana. My aunt Marcy was a delivery nurse and an exquisite quilt maker who taught me how to make my first quilt. I spent hours quilting, and using the embroidery skills my grandmother had taught me to sew flowers all over my denim shirt that summer. I also began to collect antiques, one of which was a patchwork jacket made from an old quilt.

That fall I began attending a new school in Oregon, but at the time only polyester dresses were worn, a far cry from my quilted jacket and embroidered jean shirt. I was a prime target for teasing and came home in tears, but I remember finding refuge in my patchwork quilt, a place where I had begun building the world in which I wanted to live.

In my early twenties I continued to create the world I wanted by living in a log cabin in the Santa Cruz Mountains of California, where I raised goats, chickens, a faithful dog named Jessie, and a garden filled with rabbits. Like Minna, I also sang to one of the goats when she was in labor and saw the little hooves sticking out, so I finally just pulled on them and delivered a kid!

While living in California, I heard a country song on the radio called "Coat of Many Colors," sung by Emmylou Harris and written by Dolly Parton. The song struck a chord in me, reminding me a bit of my own experiences, but nothing came of it until I moved to Massachusetts. There I happened to share what I vaguely remembered of the song with my editor Maria Modugno, but I added my own story and characters. Maria encouraged me to create a new story that became a picture book called *The Rag Coat*, which was published in 1991.

The Rag Coat has remained in print since its publication, and over the years I have received letters from schoolchildren asking for another book that shows Lottie becoming "nicer." *The Rag Coat* was performed as a ballet at the University of Utah and has also been considered for treatment as an opera and as a screenplay for film. Encouraged by all of these requests and interest, I thought it would be a wonderful challenge to delve deeper into Minna's world and expand the story into a novel, one where I could write all about what I love.

A Note About the Songs

The songs in *Minna's Patchwork Coat* are favorites that my husband and I sang with our daughter when she was a child. As I began my research into these folk songs, I discovered that most have no known author or date of origin. Just as the Grimm brothers collected fairy tales in Germany by listening to the stories, people passed down songs, games, and dances orally, too. I also discovered that some songs were known as "play party songs," which were developed in the nineteenth century by young people in areas where dancing was forbidden. But many songs were not written down until much later. I've done my best to find the earliest publications of these songs, as I wanted to use the versions closest to what would have been sung in Appalachia in the early twentieth century, when Minna's story takes place.

Many Appalachian songs and dances were first collected and printed by British music teacher Cecil Sharp (1859–1924), who noted nearly five thousand tunes in all, including nearly three thousand songs from England and more than fifteen hundred from the Appalachian Mountains. Sharp founded the English Folk Dance

Society in London in 1911, and a branch of that organization, the Country Dance and Song Society, was founded in the United States in 1915. When I could not find a written origin of the play party song "Great Big House in New Orleans," the members of the society bent over backward to help me in my research and to secure permission from the earliest known publisher. I wish to express great gratitude to Dr. John Ramsay; Patty Tarter; David Millstone; Jeff Martell; Dr. John M. Feierabend, professor of music at the Hartt School of Music; Carole Lubrowski and Christine Bird, librarians at the University of Hartford; and Maryke Barber, librarian at Hollins University. I especially want to thank Bruce Greene, director of World Around Songs, for kindly granting permission to publish the lyrics for "Great Big House" in *Minna's Patchwork Coat*.

I am also grateful to the Seeger family, who collected many modern versions of the folk songs in this book. Readers may want to explore Mike and Peggy Seeger's audio recordings and refer to Ruth Crawford Seeger's book *American Folk Songs for Children* (Doubleday and Company, 1948).

"**All Through the Night**" (page 267): The earliest known publication was in Welsh in 1784 in *Musical and Poetical Relics of the Welsh Bards*. In

1884, Sir Harold Boulton wrote the English lyrics that are most widely used today and are found in part in *140 Folk Songs with Piano Accompaniment, "Rote Songs" for Grades I, II and III* by Dr. Archibald T. Davison and Thomas Whitney Surette (E. C. Schirmer Music Company, 1921).

"The Ash Grove" (page 62): An early Welsh version was published in 1862 in Volume I of *Welsh Melodies, With Welsh And English Poetry* by John Thomas the harpist, with Welsh words by John Jones (also known as Talhaiarn) and English words by Thomas Oliphant. However, the best-known version was written in English by John Oxenford in the nineteenth century and published in part in *One Hundred Folk Songs From All Nations* (Oliver Ditson Company, 1911).

"Betty Botter" (page 163): This tongue twister was originally written by Carolyn Wells and was first published in *The Jingle Book* (Macmillan, 1899).

"Great Big House in New Orleans" (page 154): A Southern play party song with an unknown author, the first published version was collected by Lynn Rohrbough from singer Neva Mae Tom in Columbus, Ohio, and was published by Cooperative Recreation Service (now known as World Around Song) in 1940 in the *Handy Play Party Book.*

"Hush, Little Baby" (or "The Mockingbird Song") (page 23): This American folk song has no known author. There are many versions of it, and singers would often add their own lines and names. The earliest known publication date is 1918 in the Cecil Sharp Manuscript Collection, from performer Mrs. Julie Boone.

"The Journey of the Leaves" (or "Come Away") (page 103): This German folk song was translated into English by Homer H. Harbour and can be found in *140 Folk Songs with Piano Accompaniment, "Rote Songs" for Grades I, II and III* by Dr. Archibald T. Davison and Thomas Whitney Surette (E. C. Schirmer Music Company, 1921).

"Little Bird, Little Bird" (page 19): This song and game has several variations and has been sung in many regions and countries. I used most of the lyrics found in Robert Ford's *Children's Rhymes, Children's Games, Children's Songs, Children's Stories* (Alexander Gardner, 1904).

"This Old Man" (page 95): There is no known author, and this song was sung in England and the United States with a variety of lyrics. It is a part of the *Cecil Sharp Manuscript Collection*, and a similar version was included in Cecil Sharp and Sabine Baring-Gould's *English Folk-Songs for Schools* in 1906.

"Who Built the Ark?" (page 96): This American folk song has no known author. The lyrics vary, and it can be found in *Twenty Kentucky Mountain Songs*, with words collected by Lorraine Wyman and melodies collected by Howard Brockway (Oliver Ditson Company, 1920).

It Takes a Whole Lot of People
to Make a Book

In the midst of writing and illustrating this novel, I was spending summers teaching drawing in the Children's Book Writing and Illustrating MFA program at Hollins University in Roanoke, Virginia, which gave me the perfect opportunity to do further research on Appalachian culture. I audited Dr. Tina L. Hanlon's class Appalachian Traditions and Adaptations in Children's Literature, and I thank her for sharing many of her books and films and for bringing me to the Exhibition Coal Mine in Beckley, West Virginia. I also visited the Youth Museum and the Mountain Homestead, which provided pictorial reference information on the church, some of the log cabins, and the classroom.

Some of the herbal information comes from my recent research on Appalachian and specifically Cherokee herbal medicines, but much of it comes from my years of training with herbalists, especially Rosemary Gladstar and the teachers at her New England Women's Herbal Conference, as well as my studies with Native American healers and shamans of plant spirit medicine.

The Foxfire books, a classic series consisting of high school students' interviews of Appalachian people sharing their memories and "affairs of plain living," were of great help. They hold a wealth of information on the crafts and lore of the Appalachian region. *The Cherokee* (Lifeways series), by Raymond Bial, and *The Cherokee* (First Americans series), by Sarah De Capua, were also helpful books on Cherokee traditions. I am grateful to John Rice Irwin, founder of the Museum of Appalachia, for reading *The Rag Coat* for historical accuracy years earlier. Mr. Irwin's book *A People and Their Quilts* was one of the most useful texts on quilting that I consulted. Some of the patterns he discusses were used as inspiration for the chapter titles in *Minna's Patchwork Coat*.

The school I used as a model for the Rabbit Ridge School is the Nash Hill School, built in 1786 in Williamsburg, Massachusetts. I am grateful to my friends, the Marti and Black families, for preserving this school on their property, and specifically to Penelope (Souci), Charlotte (Lottie), and Hannah, Olivia, and Sherrie (Quilting Mothers) for posing as many of the characters and supplying their chickens, garden, old stove, and family quilt as handy references.

I also wish to thank the Hartsbrook School for allowing me access to their goats, lambs, chickens, sheep, and playground, where many of the children and their parents acted out the scenes. I am indebted to all of the other expert actors who have helped make the book come alive, including Alexandra Irvine (as the perfect Minna); her mother, Anna Maria (Aunt Nora); Alexandra's father, Peter (Minna's papa); Alexandra's grandpa John F. Nygren (Clyde's grandpa); Talon Neville (Lester); Jasper Piermarini (Shane); Sara Rose Page (Minna's mama); her daughters, Arya Rose and Layla Grace Page (younger children); Bisbee Hooper and Henry Lax-Holmes (Clemmie); Sophia Lax-Holmes (younger girl); Jonah Toran (Clyde); his sister, Ilana (younger girl); Stephen Katz (Shane's father); and Louise Chicoine (Miss Campbell).

While I was working on the drawings, I listened to lots of bluegrass music and wore clothing similar to what would have been worn during this time period, supplied to me by Magnolia Pearl, a unique company in Texas. Robin Brown's designs include clothing handmade from homespun linen, vintage lace, embroidery, and even patches! I thank Faith Scott, who sent boxes of treasures for me to use as inspiration for the characters' attire. I named the goats Magnolia and Pearl in gratitude.

I also want to thank the many people at Little, Brown Books for Young Readers for their wonderful work on this book, especially my insightful and encouraging editors, Andrea Spooner and Deirdre Jones, not only for their expert guidance but also for allowing me to find my voice. I also thank senior designer Liz Casal, copy editor Erica Stahler, and production editor Barbara Bakowski for their expertise.

I thank my encouraging writing buddies: Dixie Brown, Barbara Goldin, Amy Gordon, Dennis Nolan, Roberta Jones, Grace LeClair, and Suzanne Smith.

I thank my artist friend Koo Schadler, who knows the secret of illuminating the lights against the darks.

I thank Dolly Parton for her inspiring song "Coat of Many Colors."

I thank my parents for giving me an understanding of the soft stuffing that is inside *Minna's Patchwork Coat*; Aunt Marcy (after whom I named Minna's mama) for instilling in me a love of quilts; Nana for giving me a love of embroidery and the hills of West Virginia; and my sister, Brookie, who encouraged me to climb my own mountain and who tried her best to hike the entire Appalachian Trail from Georgia to Maine.

Most of all I thank my partner, Dennis Nolan, for always being there in the most helpful, loving, patient, and wise way a body could be.

About This Book

The cover was painted in oil, and the interior illustrations were rendered in graphite pencil on Arches paper. This book was edited by Andrea Spooner and Deirdre Jones and designed by Liz Casal and Tracy Shaw with art direction by Sasha Illingworth and Dave Caplan. The production was supervised by Erika Schwartz, and the production editor was Barbara Bakowski. This book was printed on 45-pound Norbrite Recycled FSC cream. The text was set in Centaur, and the display type is Brandywine.

About the Author

Lauren A. Mills is the award-winning author and illustrator of *The Rag Coat* and *The Goblin Baby*, and the author of *Fairy Wings*, *Fia and the Imp*, and *The Dog Prince*, all of which she co-illustrated with her husband, Dennis Nolan. Her work has been exhibited in galleries and museums across the country, including the National Museum of Women in the Arts. Her stories have been performed by storytellers and actors across the country and on the radio, and *The Rag Coat* was performed as a ballet by the University of Utah. Mills is a visiting associate professor of drawing in the Children's Book Writing and Illustrating MFA program at Hollins University in Roanoke, Virginia. She invites you to visit her website at LaurenMillsArt.com.